MW00412581

CRESCENDO

CRESCENDO

TERRY J. MOYER

COPYRIGHT © 1995 BY
HORIZON PUBLISHERS & DISTRIBUTORS, INC.

All rights reserved, Reproduction in whole or any
parts thereof in any form or by any media without
written persmssion is prohibited.

First Printing, July 1995

International Standard Book Number
0-88290-527-9

Horizon Publishers' Catalog and Order Number
1059

Printed and distrubuted
in the United States of America by

Horizon
Publishers
& Distributors, Incorporated
P.O. Box 490 Bountiful, Utah 84011-0490

Dedication

This book is dedicated to Mr. Ervin Lesser, Maestro, musician, educator extraordinary, role model, gentleman, friend. And to all the Andrews and to all the Julies in all the high schools everywhere, whatever their names may be.

Contents

Introduction

This story and the events described in this book are fictional. It is true, of course, that there is an Oregon City High School in Oregon City, thirteen miles south of Portland, Oregon. It is true that one year in the 1950s the Oregon City High School Concert Band performed the *Finale* of Shostakovich's Fifth Symphony and "took State." Otherwise, the events described in this book are fictional.

For many years, the Oregon City High School Band was led by Mr. Ervin Lesser, a genius at working with young musicians, and a man who, to the author's knowledge, never did or said anything which was hurtful to any of his students in any way. All of the other characters are fictitious, and any resemblance between them and persons living or dead is entirely coincidental.

1
The List

Tuesday, December 1; fourth period

For the tenth time since the tardy bell had rung, Julie Ryckman looked at the top drawer of the file cabinet. For the tenth time she wondered if she would ever get a look inside it. For the tenth time she wished that Mr. Cochran and Mrs. Brandon would leave the office for a few minutes.

A few minutes should be plenty, she thought to herself. All I need is a glance at the Master Roster of Students.

Granted, the roster was confidential, and for good reason. It listed who had what grade point average, who was on report for discipline, who had been held back a grade, and a lot more. It certainly was not the sort of thing that a senior girl working fourth period in the attendance office at Oregon City High School would be allowed to see.

But Julie Ryckman had a problem, and the only apparent solution was in the Master Roster. Besides, it wasn't as if she were looking for the really *juicy* stuff anyway. Granted, an intelligent senior girl with top grades probably could figure some things out just by looking. But Julie wanted to be sure. She had to *know* which boys were taller than six feet.

At last Mr. Cochran left the office for his meeting at the district office. At last Mrs. Brandon left to make a fresh pot of coffee in the faculty lounge.

"Well, Julie," she said aloud, "this is your chance. It's now or never!" Trying to act casual, she walked to the file cabinet. In her hand she held the day's attendance report—just in case Mrs. Brandon returned and asked why Julie had the top drawer open. Quickly, she removed the file marked MASTER ROSTER, and opened it.

Let's see. Four-hundred-ninety-two students. All names alphabetical by grade. Better look at the seniors first. Everything tabulated: names, addresses, phone numbers, birth dates and places, grade point averages. Aha! Height! I'll check the Class of '54 boys first.

Julie's finger moved swiftly down the "height" column as she wrote the names of four senior boys. Next to the names she listed their heights:

JENNINGS, Ronald V.   6'-2"

LARSEN, Arch   6'-1 1/2"

McKINLEY, Sherman R.   6'-0"

SHERWOOD, Andrew   6'-3"

Only four senior boys? thought Julie. This is worse than I thought. I'd better have a look at the Class of '55.

To her list Julie now added the names of three boys in the junior class:

HECHT, Ronald R.   6'-1/2"

STEPHENSEN, Jack   6'-0"

WEILER, Jonathan C.   6'-1"

Do I really want to add *sophomores* to this list? Julie asked herself. Then she turned to the roster of the Class of '56, where she found two more tall boys:

PAGE, Allen D.   6'-2 1/2"

JERGENSEN, Miles A.   6'-4"

Tall timber in that forest, she mused. But they *are* sophomores, after all.

Just out of curiosity, Julie checked the Class of '57, and found two boys who could just make the cut:

FOSBERG, Robert V.   6'-0"

WATSON, Thomas   6'-0"

Mrs. Brandon still hadn't returned. Though she knew what the answer would be, Julie took time to run her finger down the "height" column once more. It was just as she had suspected: There was only *one* girl at Oregon City High School who stood six feet tall.

Thursday, December 3; first period

In the band room Julie opened her instrument case and began assembling her oboe. Four years ago, while still living in Michigan, she had started on the flute. But the band director there had needed an oboe player, and he had asked Julie to make the switch.

It hadn't been hard. Julie was considered a smart girl, and she had a lot of talent in music. Her parents had bought her a beautiful new instrument, and then had paid for lessons for her. The band director in Ann Arbor told her she had become one of the best.

Then three major catastrophes occurred. First, and worst of all, Julie's Mom died, leaving Julie to take care of the cooking, the cleaning, the laundry and all the shopping for herself and her grieving father.

Next, her dad decided to move to Oregon to be closer to his married daughter and grandchildren. Julie had had to say good-bye to all her friends at Ann Arbor High.

Then right after they had arrived in Oregon City came the growth spurt. Taller and relentlessly taller she grew. Finally, near the end of her sophomore year at Oregon City High, her growth slowed and then stopped, leaving Julie Ryckman a dead even six feet tall.

Six feet tall. Seventy-two inches tall—a sophomore girl towering above all the other girls and almost all of the boys. Now here she was a senior, and still the tallest tree in the forest.

Julie took the wet double reed from her mouth and fitted it to the upper end of her oboe. She took her seat next to Arlene Simmons, Oregon City High School's one and only bassoon player.

Julie thought about Arlene: five-foot-three, pretty, wealthy, popular with the boys, a spoiled brat.

Five-foot-three, she thought. Wouldn't it be nice to be shorter than *every* boy in school! Small wonder Arlene had a date for every dance, every football game, every party.

Ruefully, Julie recalled that once she, too, had been five-foot-three, tiny and pretty, and eagerly looking forward to dating every boy in Michigan. Now she was six-feet tall and a senior. And while she was prettier than ever, she was still waiting for her first date.

The tallest girl at Oregon City High School looked again at Arlene Simmons and tried very hard not to hate her.

Friday, December 4; afternoon

Julie listed all eleven boys in order of height and started on some research. By Friday afternoon, her list had been reduced to two, the first to go had been the two freshmen: number 10, Bob Fosburg, and number 11, Tom Watson. Tall or not, they were still freshmen, and no senior girl anywhere could be seen in public with a freshman boy.

A small amount of research had revealed that Number 1, Don Jennings; Number 3, Sherm McKinley; and Number 5, Ron Hecht, all were going steady with shorter girls who should have been dating shorter boys.

Julie lined out Number 2, Arch Larsen, when she learned that he had jumped out of school in favor of jumping out of airplanes. Being at Fort Benning was a definite drawback in the Julie Ryckman Sweepstakes.

Julie dropped three more boys from her list because they turned out to be certified creeps. The girls who had dated Number 6, Jack Stephensen, referred to him as the "The Wrestling Octopus." Similarly, Number 9, Miles Jergensen, was reported to be a party man given to heavy drinking and beating up on girlfriends. And as for Number 8, Allen Page, he was so stuck on himself that no girl could stand to go out with him twice. Julie wasn't *that* desperate. (And besides, he was a sophomore.)

That left only two eligible tall boys on the list: Number 4, Andrew Sherwood, and Number 7, Jon Weiler. And tonight's football game with West Linn would give Julie a good chance to observe each up fairly closely.

Jon Weiler had several things going for him: he was not only tall, he was handsome, with a deep cleft in his chin. Beyond that, Jon was a good student—and popular—and an authentic football hero in a school with almost no football heroes. But at the pep rally Julie observed that one of the cheerleaders was wearing Jon Weiler's letterman jacket—a sure sign that he was off limits, at least for now.

In her mind, Julie scratched Number 7 from her list. One more tall boy snapped up by some miserable little cupie doll not tall enough to kiss him on his handsome cleft chin! One fewer tall boy available for the tallest girl in school.

"Julie," she said to herself, "I hope we don't have to scratch any more boys from this list, because there is only one boy left. And his name is Number Four."

2
The Boy

The same evening; later

Julie had known "Number Four" for a couple of years. She and all the other girls in school knew that "Number Four" was tall, good-looking, and intelligent. Every girl in school knew that he had a powerful, muscular build. They could see that he ought to be an outstanding football player, or basketball player, or wrestler, or anything else. And they all knew that he had turned down both Coach Ellis and Coach Shelton for every team.

Julie knew that other girls had shown an interest in "Number Four" and then had given up on him. They had all had the same experience: he had stuttered and stammered and blushed and then had gone into hiding. Every girl who had tried to get something started with "Number Four" told the same story: a panicky look; no conversation; no dates; no tall, well-built boyfriend. It was already common knowledge among the girls at Oregon City High School that "Number Four" was completely hopeless.

And not one of them had a notion why.

Julie Ryckman had heard all these stories, and for three years now she had assumed that Andrew Sherwood really was hopeless. She had "seen" him all right—in band and in the halls and around school ever since she had moved in from Michigan. She had even been in a few classes with him. But tonight at the West Linn game she was "seeing" him with new eyes. If not a single other tall boy was available, then maybe . . . .

All through the game Julie quietly watched "Number Four." What she saw she had seen before, had heard about from the other girls. Andrew Sherwood was genuinely good looking. He had shiny brown hair and deep blue eyes. His powerful shoulders and arms ran down to strong, angular hands.

But what the other girls had said was true: Number Four seemed unable to look at girls, or boys for that matter, in the eyes. He never joined in conversations and seemed hardly to have a voice. In fact, Julie couldn't recall ever having heard him speak—and she had been around him for three years.

Why? she asked herself. Why won't he talk to a girl? What's he afraid of? Why does a tall, handsome boy act as if he had leprosy? And then the other more pressing question: Is he *really* hopeless?

As usual, the football game went badly. With arch-rival West Linn High in town for their annual grudge match, hopes had been high that somehow Oregon City might pull out a victory this year, but it was not to be. Again this year—as in most years—West Linn humiliated Oregon City. The scoreboard told the sorry story: West Linn 63, Oregon City 0. The season ended with Oregon City High having lost all nine of its games.

The defeated team left the field looking like drowned dogs. The Oregon City fans, and especially the band members, left the grandstand as depressed as the gloomy overcast weather. The West Linn fans managed to show both their joy at winning and their scorn for Oregon City, whom they taunted as "the world's all-time losers."

As Julie put away her instrument, she watched Andrew Sherwood. He quickly put his sax in its case, then headed for the exit. Following from a distance, Julie made some mental notes. He spoke to no one. No friends were waiting to meet him. He walked briskly away from Kelly Field east, toward Redland Road.

"Andrew Sherwood," she said under her breath, "why do you walk home alone in the rain? Where do you live? Do you have a friend? What kind of person are you? And are *you* the boy who's going with me on my first date?"

The same evening, after the ball game

At the junction of Redland Road, Andrew Sherwood continued walking. Each time car headlights appeared, he put out one thumb, hoping to hitch a ride. Drivers hurrying home through the mist saw a tall, well-built farm-boy wearing a red and white band uniform which didn't quite cover his wrists and ankles. A closer look might have revealed battered, unpolished shoes and powerful hands well decorated with callouses and scars. Anyone passing the tall farm boy on the side of the road would have described him as good-looking—that is, anyone except the boy himself.

Several vehicles appeared out of the darkness, then hurried past the walking boy in the band uniform. At length, the lights of one more vehicle appeared. An ancient farm truck pulled to a stop.

"How far you going, Son?"

"I live a mile down Ferguson Road."

"Ma and I can get you and your fiddle to Ferguson Road, if you like. Hop in the back."

"Thanks!" said Andrew, loading his instrument case into the enclosed truck, and hopping in.

As the truck began moving, Andrew opened the case, and assembled the tenor sax. Leaning against the cab of the truck, he stretched his feet out before him. His eyes closed, he began to play a rich, warm blues tune; it was mellow in the low register, soft and mournful.

Neither the driver nor his wife heard the music behind them over the noise of the engine. Not a soul heard the beautiful music except the tall, painfully shy farm boy who was speaking his true feelings through a tenor saxophone:

> You ain't been blue: No, no, no.
> You ain't been blue, 'til you've had that mood indigo.
> That feelin' goes stealin' down to my shoes
> While I sit and sing, 'Go 'long blues.'

Andrew didn't know the words. He didn't know that the song was already decades old. He was only involved in the mood, the music, the feel of a good song custom-made for a lonely person and a tenor sax.

> Always get that mood indigo,
> Since my baby said good-bye.
> In the evenin' when lights are low,
> I'm so lonesome I could cry.

There were things a shy person like Andrew couldn't say, feelings he couldn't talk about out loud. To him, there were things a tenor sax could say so much better than he could.

'Cause there's nobody who cares about me.
I'm just a soul who's bluer than blue can be.
When I get that mood indigo,
I could lay me down and die.

The farm truck slowed to a stop at the junction with Ferguson Road. Andrew put his tenor back into its case and shouted thanks to the driver for the lift. He vaulted easily from the truck to the road, then lifted down the worn saxophone case marked "PROPERTY OF O.C.H.S."

Soon the truck was gone, and Andrew began walking down a dark gravel road. Straight ahead he could see the narrow gap in the black wall of fir trees where the road cut through the forest. To his left and right, occasional clearings marked small farmsteads and pastures. Lights shone from some of the houses.

As he walked, Andrew talked to himself out loud in a confident voice, with no trace of stammering or stuttering. "Stupid football team. We never win *anything*. We never even come close. So what's new about that? We lost every game last year, too, didn't we? And the year before that. Truth is, we haven't won a game since Lewis and Clark were here sitting in the grandstand, and what'll you bet they were cheering for West Linn."

After fifteen minutes, Andrew arrived at the edge of the plateau, where the road drops steeply toward Abernathy Creek. He opened the battered mailbox identified with the name SHERWOOD, found nothing, and closed it.

"Bad news," he said out loud. "Someone's picked up the mail. The Old Man must be home. And neither cow has been milked yet!" Andrew quickened his pace.

Halfway down the hill, at a sharp curve, the road opened into a clearing in the forest, revealing an old two-story farmhouse, a small barn, a three-acre pasture, a chicken coop, a garden, and several young fruit trees.

At the end of the driveway Andrew stopped, puzzled. "The pickup isn't here. Maybe Ma walked up the hill and got the mail. Maybe the Old Man is still at Coney Island Bar having a few. Maybe I can get out of this after all."

Quietly, Andrew climbed the stone steps to the porch, and opened the front door of the old farmhouse.

At the door he was met by his mother, a tall, kindly woman with a gentle but careworn face. Her arms around him, she said gently, "I'm glad you got home all right, Son. Did you have a nice time at the ball game?"

"We lost again."

As Alice Sherwood smiled, her face looked younger. "I'm glad you were able to be with your friends for a little while."

Gently, Andrew disengaged himself from his mother's embrace. "Ma, I've got to go milk the cows."

"Yes. That's right. Your Pa will be here soon. I'll warm some supper in the oven for you."

Andrew hung up his band hat and coat on the enclosed porch. Then he put on his work coat, picked up the flashlight and the two milk buckets, and walked toward the barn.

Saturday, December 5; afternoon

It was the sort of cold, dreary, rainy, awful day which Clackamas County, Oregon, had patented and made famous. Clouds of battleship gray in a lowering sky continued to pour rain upon the already soggy landscape. It was a wonderful day to remain indoors.

But Andrew Sherwood and his father spent the entire day outdoors, trying to remove a huge stump from the pasture.

Jim Sherwood placed a heavy steel bar under one exposed root and lifted with all his might. "Now, Son . . . with the axe!"

Andrew raised the heavy double-bladed axe high over his head, then brought it down with a powerful blow on the thick root. "Idiot!" his father screamed. "Cut *through* the root! How long do you think I can hold this stupid thing?"

Andrew raised the axe again, and again brought it down hard on the root. A large piece of root wood flew away, revealing a deep "V." Twice more the axe fell before the root was severed from the large Douglas fir stump.

Jim Sherwood sneered with contempt. "I coulda cut through that root with one stroke." He threw the shovel to Andrew. "Now dig around that next root, and let's get this stump out of this hole."

Standing ankle deep in mud, Andrew began throwing the heavy wet dirt up out of the pit, exposing yet another large root. This time his father took the axe while Andrew lifted up on the root with the steel bar. "Hold 'er there!" the older man grunted. "Hold 'er!" Then he brought the axe down on a slicing angle—and through the root.

"There," said Andrew's father with sneering satisfaction. "You see? Hit the root your way, and you need four blows. Hit the root at an angle, and you can cut clean through with one whack. You got that, Dunce?"

"Yeah, Pa." Andrew tried to wipe the rain and sweat off his face, and succeeded only in smearing mud on his forehead.

"Couple more roots, and we'll try to yank that blasted stump out with the block and tackle." The older man took the shovel and lowered himself into the muddy hole surrounding the stump. Quickly, efficiently, he removed dirt and mud from around the next root.

"I think we're ready," said the older man. "Remember, hit the root on an angle. . . ."

With powerful arms and shoulders, Andrew raised the heavy axe high and started to bring it down. But one foot slipped in the mud, and the axe hit the root at a shallow angle. The head of the axe skipped off the root and into the steel bar held by Jim Sherwood.

"You stupid idiot!" shrieked Andrew's father. "Can't you do *anything* right? Seventeen years old and you still don't know how to handle an axe? Who told you to use an axe on a steel bar, you stupid ox?"

"Pa, I'm sorry. My foot slipped and I . . . ."

His father was furious. "Your foot slipped? Well you ought to know by now that you don't swing a stupid axe until your clumsy feet are set firm. Haven't I told you that a thousand times? You stupid, clumsy ox! It'll be a miracle if that axe ain't ruined! I need a son to work alongside me, and the good Lord gives me a lazy, clumsy, good-for-nothin' bonehead. . . ."

The rain fell harder, but Andrew didn't notice. He kept his silence, knowing that eventually the raging storm of his father's anger would subside.

"Now, Idiot: let's try it again. And this time try to keep from chopping on the steel bar, all right?"

Again Andrew's father lifted up on the root with the bar. Again Andrew wrought a massive stroke. This time the axe sliced cleanly through the large root in one blow. His massive blow was driven as much by silent anger as by strength.

"Let's rig the block and tackle," said the older man. "Maybe we can tilt that stump up out of that hole . . . ."

Andrew attached a steel hook to the choker cable looped around the trunk of a nearby tree while his father ran another choker around the stump and under some of the roots on the far side. Then father and son braced their feet and began pulling in unison on the heavy rope.

Again and again they pulled, father and son straining with all their strength, and the remaining roots refusing to let the stump go. Straining muscles appeared in Andrew's neck and face, and the rain and the sweat ran down into his eyes.

And then the steel hook attached to the choker came loose, and the rope and tackle blocks went flying. Both Andrew and his father fell heavily to the wet ground.

"Well, what in tarnation was *that*?" roared Andrew's father. "You set the stupid choker wrong, you idiot! Doesn't the dumbest ape in the Portland Zoo know you have to put the hook through *both* loops of the choker?"

"Pa, I'm sure I set the . . . ."

"Shut up! I can't believe what a trial and a burden it is, working with a kid who is big and dumb and stupid and ugly! One of these days you're going to get me killed!"

"Pa, I'm . . . ."

"Don't tell me what you are!" roared Jim. "I know already! You're lazy! You're stupid! You're dumb! You're a jackass! You're useless!"

Andrew stood silent, unable to defend himself, unable to escape the abuse being rained upon him. Though Andrew was a full six inches taller than his father, it was no longer in the boy's nature to protest or resist. For seventeen years the father had dominated and cursed and ridiculed and abused his son, and Andrew had learned well that he had only one option: to keep his silence.

Besides, didn't all fathers treat their sons this way?

"Now get your lazy butt down in that pit and dig out some more roots. Maybe you're just barely smart enough to run a shovel and not get somebody killed . . . ."

Another hour passed. Shovel. Mud. "Stupid moron!" Steel bar. Axe. Sweat. "Lazy butt-head!" Clothes wet through to the skin. Block and tackle. More mud. Endless rain. "Stupid jackass!"

From time to time Andrew's mind escaped. Was it really true that other teenagers went to the movies on a Saturday? Was there really such a thing as shooting free throws on somebody's driveway? Were there radio programs and movies on a Saturday afternoon? Was there such a thing as wearing nice clothes and relaxing in a warm room while talking with a girlfriend on the telephone? Did other kids go shopping with their friends? Did other guys work on cars together?

Two hours later the huge stump remained firmly attached to Clackamas County. Andrew ventured to speak: "Pa? Can we take a break? Maybe get a drink?"

Reluctantly, his father nodded, wiping sweat and rain from his face. The man and his son retreated to the non-protection of the nearby woods. Each man drank deeply from the water in the fruit jar, then sat down at the base of a huge tree and stared vacantly at the offending stump in the pasture.

Andrew sneaked a glance at his father. What he saw was a man much shorter than himself, with gray at his temples and in his beard stubble. The man's blue eyes were barely visible because of a habitual squint acquired from working outdoors every day.

"Somethin' eatin' on you, Boy?"

"I'm all right, Pa."

There was an angry set to the jaw, a certain grimness about the mouth. "Too much band and too much football is how I read it," said the older man.

Quietly, not daring to look directly at his father, Andrew said, "Pa . . . I'm in the band. They need me. If . . . if I'm not there, my grade goes down . . . ."

"Band grades don't make no never mind, Boy. School is for learnin' how to work—not for foolin' around. I reckon you need less band and more stumps."

Andrew had been learning for seventeen years that it was no good arguing with this man. "Yes, Pa." There was a long silence before Andrew spoke again:

"Pa? I'm so wet and tired . . . . Couldn't we knock it off for today? Maybe root this stump out next Saturday?"

There was contempt on Jim Sherwood's face and in his voice. "Boy, you win the prize for the laziest kid in the county! You ain't never gonna amount to *nothin'* til you learn how to work. We'll quit when that stump is layin' on its back!"

Andrew took a deep breath, then silently let it and his hopes go. The rain fell harder as the two arose and returned to the stump in the pasture.

"Someday, Son, you'll thank me. You'll see. So help me, I am gonna teach you how to *work!*"

Wet through to the skin, Andrew took the shovel and slogged back into the ankle-deep mud around the stump as the rain continued.

Sunday, December 6: late evening

Ervin Lesser stepped to the podium. Dressed in formal white tie and tails, he turned to acknowledge the fervent applause of the crowd. As usual, he bowed first to the left, then to the right, then stood with both arms extended outward, thanking his adoring fans. "Thank you," he murmured. "Thank you."

As the applause died away, he turned to his orchestra, and picked up the long, slender baton from the music stand before him. In perfect unison, the members of the orchestra lifted their instruments even as he lifted his baton.

Maestro Lesser signalled the orchestra with an upbeat, and the Finale of Shostakovich's magnificent Fifth Symphony was under way. The opening whole note swelled to *fortissimo* before the brasses sounded the main theme. Then the entire orchestra entered with four slashing eighth notes on the beat.

The strings and high woodwinds picked up the glorious music, sounding like a musical blizzard blowing out of Twentieth Century Russia. The brasses and lower woodwinds repeated and paraphrased the strings' and flutes' powerful moving lines.

"Wonderful," he thought. "Magnificent." The New York Philharmonic had never been so responsive, so crisp, so precise as it was tonight. His musicians knew the music, knew their conductor, knew what he wanted from them, and gave it all willingly, joyfully, perfectly.

Ten minutes into the *Finale*, the Maestro was overwhelmed with the beauty of it all. Placing his baton on the music stand, the great maestro let his New York Philharmonic continue without direction. He closed his eyes and lifted his face, then put his hands in his pockets. Musician, conductor, maestro extraordinaire, acclaimed trumpet virtuoso, he now became one with his audience. With all the others in the great hall, Ervin Lesser permitted himself to be transported by the genius of Shostakovich and the incomparable glory of the New York Philharmonic.

The *Finale* was nearing its conclusion. Maestro Lesser picked up his baton and returned to his work. A listener no more, he drew from his orchestra a flawless ending for the flawless *Finale* of Shostakovich's Symphony Number Five.

The audience in Avery Fisher Hall leapt to its feet and burst into wild applause and spontaneous shouts of "Bravo! Bravo!"

Bowing deeply, then asking his orchestra to rise, Ervin Lesser basked in the adulation of the crowd. Triumphantly, he walked off the stage.

And into drab reality. He lifted the needle from the record, and switched off the power. Once again he was in the modest living room of a modest house on a modest street in Oregon City, Oregon, a million miles from Symphony Hall in New York City.

"A bachelor of arts degree. A master's degree," he murmured to himself. "And for what? So I could teach elementary school music in Ashland—and high school band in Oregon City? Shall I spend my whole life listening to squeaking clarinets and squawking saxophones? Shall I never have a great orchestra of my own to conduct?"

Carefully, slowly, Mr. Lesser took off his white tie and black tails, and put them back in their clothes bag in the tiny bedroom closet. Slowly, wearily, he put on his pajamas and climbed into bed. He turned off the light and fell into a restless sleep.

3
The Decision

Monday, December 7; before school

A half hour before school on Monday morning Arlene Simmons wheeled her red T-Bird into the student parking lot across the street from Oregon City High. She greeted several friends, then took from the back seat several books plus the cymbals she had played at Friday night's football game.

As she entered the main hallway of the old red-brick building she came upon the previous week's pre-game banners, long paper strips taped to the walls. Arlene stood before each banner in turn and angrily shouted the hopeful message printed there.

"BEAT WEST LINN!" she read loudly as she ripped the banner from the wall.

"THIS TIME FOR SURE! Right! This time we lose for sure!" she stormed.

"LEAN ON THE LIONS! Ha! We really leaned on them, didn't we?"

Angrily, she kicked and tossed the paper banners, then stalked down the hallway toward her locker. On the way, she passed a large, nearly empty trophy case.

Still furious, Arlene opened her locker and threw her books inside. Then, cymbals in hand, she entered the nearby band room. "Four years at this school, and we've never won *anything*! Losers! Losers! Losers!" she shouted at everyone in the room and at no one in particular. "Stupid football team! Stupid baseball team! Stupid track team! Losers, every one of them!"

The other band members were used to this. Each Friday night the band watched the Pioneers get beat. Each Monday morning Arlene threw a tantrum. There were some things in life you could always count on.

As Arlene's fury ebbed, Wally Arnold continued tuning his two ancient tympani drums. Carol Larsen continued tuning her flute. Chuck Walton continued polishing his new cornet. Darryl Jepson continued practicing hot licks on his clarinet.

Through all of this, Andrew Sherwood sat in a corner studying his physics textbook. And Julie Ryckman studied Andrew.

Monday, December 7; first period

As the tardy bell rang, the would-be conductor of the New York Philharmonic entered the band room. Short in stature, with black curly hair and neatly-trimmed mustache, he looked every bit the perfectionist band director and musician that he was.

Still in his first semester as a teacher at Oregon City High, Mr. Lesser already had come to be recognized as a very popular and highly respected teacher. A bachelor still, music was his sole interest in life. Ervin Lesser demanded the best from himself and he tolerated nothing less from the students in first period concert band. Somehow, without his ever having required it, the members of the band had come to address Mr. Lesser as "Sir."

But this Monday morning Ervin sensed that something was in the air. Even after the tardy bell had rung, several students still had not assembled their instruments, still were not ready to get down to work. He called the band to order by tapping on his music stand with his baton, and the room fell silent. "What's the problem, people?" he asked.

Chuck Walton answered for the others. "You were there, Sir. You saw what happened."

Wally Arnold translated Chuck's statement. "We lost to West Linn, Sir."

"It was a disaster," added Carole Larsen.

"Worse than that," corrected Darryl Jepson. "We were so bad, West Linn put in their junior varsity and even some of their freshmen."

"They could have put in their trombone section," agreed another.

Lee McCrory summed it up: "They could have phoned in the score and beat us without even showing up!"

Too loudly, Arlene Simmons recited her theme song once more: "So what's new? We never win *anything*! I think West Linn is right: we really *are* losers!"

"You people are a bit down on yourselves today, aren't you." Mr. Lesser's words were more statement than question. "Feeling a little sorry for yourselves, are you? Well, having someone *call* you a loser doesn't make it so."

"What would you call us, Sir?" asked Ilene Anderson.

"I'd call us a group of winners who haven't yet discovered the secret of winning."

Ilene choked out a bitter laugh. "Winners? You'd call us *winners?*"

"This is Mr. Lesser's first semester here," suggested Lee. "It takes some time to discover what world class losers we really are . . . ."

"People," began Mr. Lesser, "It looks like we need to talk more than we need to rehearse. You can put away your instruments while we talk.

"I learned as a student at Juliard that *anyone* can be a winner if he wants something badly enough to pay the price. The great musicians, the great architects, the great athletes—they're mostly rather ordinary people who wanted something badly enough to work harder than other ordinary people."

Barry Swinton, first chair tenor sax, remained skeptical. "Are you saying we could have beaten West Linn last Friday night?"

"Absolutely, if we had wanted it badly enough."

Arlene's reply came back quickly: "But we *wanted* it! We really *wanted* to beat West Linn!"

"You don't understand, Miss Simmons. Wanting it badly on Friday night isn't enough. You have to want it all summer and all fall, not just the Friday night of the game. You have to want it enough to grunt and sweat and push even when you're hot and tired or cold and hurting. You have to want it more than anything else—enough to pay the price. *Then* you can have it. Then nobody can keep it from you."

"Maybe so, but . . . ."

"No 'buts' . . . . I've seen it happen. I've done it myself. It really works. It *always* works if you are willing to pay the price."

There was a long pause as that thought sank in. Then Mr. Lesser spoke in a very quiet voice. "You people, for example. You could take first place in the annual state band competition . . . ."

There was dead silence in the room. The students looked at each other, then at Mr. Lesser, each wishing it were so, but skeptical still.

"Really, people. This band could be rated best in the State of Oregon if you wanted it enough to practice more than any other school."

"Do you really think so, Sir?" asked Carole.

"No doubt about it, Miss Larson. And not just 1-A competition against West Linn and the other small schools, mind you. If you wanted it badly enough, you could knock off the biggest high schools in the state and take the 4-A championship!"

"That would take a lot of work . . . ."

"You don't know how *much* work! Still, it remains true: If you wanted it badly enough to pay the full price, you could take State in band."

"Oregon City? State *4-A* champs? Best in State?" A few students were becoming excited by the vision of what might be.

"But not with some easy piece of fluff, mind you. We'd have to go into the competition with the meanest, toughest thing we could find—something so hard that nobody else would dare try it, let alone perform it in front of judges."

Junior Weldon exclaimed, "We can do it!"

With grim satisfaction, Arlene Simmons added, "I want to see West Linn's face when we take State 4-A!"

Mr. Lesser brought the band back to reality. "Hold on, People. We haven't beaten anybody yet. If we were to do it, it would only come after ten weeks of hard work, endless practicing, long hours of rehearsals, and strict training rules. You couldn't be state 4-A champs unless you were willing to pay the full price."

"We're willing!"

"Yeah! We can do it!"

"Of course you can!" There was a long pause before Mr. Lesser continued. "But first you need to go home and think about it. You need to be sure that your parents will support you in this. You need to talk to each other. You need to look inside yourselves and see if you really are willing to pay the price."

"You keep talking about the price . . . ."

"You want the price? Let me give it to you straight. Miss Larson, get this down in writing on the board." Mr. Lesser now laid it out while Carole wrote the training rules on the chalkboard.

Mr. Lesser spoke bluntly, grimly, minimizing nothing. "First, you'd have to attend *all* rehearsals. Absolutely no exceptions. Repeat: absolutely NO exceptions."

"No surprise there, Sir," said Lee. "It's been that way ever since you took over here last September."

Second, we would rehearse every school day before first period, just as soon as the school busses arrived."

"Hey, that's when I do my homework," said Wally.

"You'd have to find another time if we decided to go ahead with this," replied the band director.

"Third, we would eat lunch here in the band room every school day while we listened to a record of the competition piece. Then we would rehearse for the rest of the lunch period.

"Fourth, we would rehearse for one hour after school every day before we went home."

"Sir? Some of us ride busses. How would we get home?"

"I don't know. Have your folks pick you up? Catch a ride with someone who has a car? Hitch hike? Walk home? You'd have to arrange something . . . ."

"What else, Sir?" It was Carole, doing blackboard duty. "Is that it?"

"Not even close. There would be a two-hour sectional rehearsal every week night. Monday, trumpets and cornets. Tuesday, low brasses. Wednesday, percussion. Thursday it would be flutes and clarinets. Friday, the other woodwinds."

"Sir? I've got a paper route . . . ."

"You'd find a way. Sixth, everybody would have to practice the competition piece at least two hours a day at home."

Martin looked genuinely worried. "Like when, Sir? What's left?"

"Like in the afternoon . . . or at four in the morning . . . or at midnight. You'd have to figure it out. If I'm asking more than you could give, I could transfer you to first period study hall."

"Anything else, Sir?" asked Ilene.

"Yes. I would expect each of you to take private lessons if possible. I know some of you couldn't do it, but I would expect those who can afford it to do so. Any questions?"

Junior said what all were thinking. "We have other classes, too, Sir."

"Term papers . . . ."

"Homework . . . ."

"That's another thing: I would expect you to spend at least as much time at home on homework as you spend on practicing your instruments. I would expect you to carry passing grades in every other class. Beyond that, you would have to work it out with your other teachers. If there were some major problem you couldn't handle, maybe I could help by talking to them.

"People, it wouldn't be easy. I know I'd be asking a lot. But I also know that if you were each getting a million dollars to take State, you'd find a way, because you'd make this your top priority. Well, I can't pay you a million dollars. But I can promise that if you made this your top priority for the next ten weeks, you *would* take State as 4-A champs. If that were something you wanted *really* wanted you'd find a way to make it happen."

Mr. Lesser took the chalk from Carole, and wrote "NO EXCEPTIONS" beside the training rules.

"Sir? What if someone got sick?" It was Arlene Simmons again.

"They'd have to bring a note from the hospital."

The bell rang. As the students started to leave, Mr. Lesser said, "People, we'll vote first period, tomorrow. Don't vote 'yes' unless you are willing to pay the whole price and live by each and every one of these training rules."

The same evening

"Well, Daisy, what do *you* think?" Andrew continued milking the brown and white Guernsey as he waited for her reply.

"I mean, I could get to school all right for the rehearsal before first period me riding the bus and all. And eating lunch in the band room would be no big deal. I could hack that all right.

"But what about a one hour rehearsal *after* school every day? How would I work that out?" Daisy ignored the question and continued eating hay.

"If I stay after school for rehearsal, that means I miss the bus. And that means I've got seven miles to either walk or hitch hike *before* I can start on the chores and the homework.

"See, Daisy, most nights I'd probably get a ride and get home before the Old Man, because you know he's going to stop at Coney Island after work and have a few. Most nights he'd get home and find me either doing the chores or already done with them.

"But what if he got home some night before I did? What if he got home and found I wasn't there yet, and the chores hadn't been done? What if he got really chapped and yanked me out of band?

"Any ideas, Old Girl? Oh, and what about Friday nights? Mr. Lesser says we'd have a one hour rehearsal after school then a two hour wood-wind sectional later that same evening. I wouldn't have time to hitch hike home, do the chores, and then hitch hike back in time for the rehearsal.

That means I wouldn't get home until who knows when and then still have all the chores to do.

"How would I sell *that* to the Old Man?" Daisy turned and looked at the tall boy with the nearly full milk bucket between his knees.

"Of course, Friday night the Old Man cashes his paycheck, and that means more beers than most nights. And that means he gets home pretty late on most Friday nights.

"I guess a lot would depend on whether I could get lucky bumming a ride home after that late rehearsal. But the private lessons are out, right? I mean, there is just no money, and that's a fact. But I'd still have to put in two or three hours a day practicing, and I for sure don't know when I'd be able to do that."

The milking done, Andrew rose from his milk stool. He set the milk buckets aside, then released Daisy and Blossom from their stanchions. Gently, he rubbed their faces and scratched behind their ears. Their damp breath warmed his chest.

"Thanks, Girls," he said. "I knew you could help me sort all of this out. You're pretty smart for a couple of old milk cows."

The same evening, later

As she dried the last of the supper dishes, Julie Ryckman considered her reflection in the window behind the sink. What she saw was a very pretty face framed in long brown hair. She saw flashing brown eyes above high cheekbones and a chin and jawline which confirmed her European heritage.

Julie had been told often enough that she was pretty, even beautiful. She was aware of that, and took quiet pride in it. But what she was far more aware of—almost always aware of—was her height. She would have preferred to have had the pretty face reflecting back from about eight inches lower in the window.

The telephone rang. It was Julie's best friend, Carole Larsen.

"Oh, hi, Carole. No, no problem. Daddy has gone back to the newspaper office to finish up some work, and I've just gotten things put away . . . .

"Homework? No, not much . . . . No, nothing for algebra, and only a couple of paragraphs for English Comp. I got most of it done at school.

"Mr. Lesser? Taking State in band? Wouldn't that be something! Well, of course we could do it! It's like Mr. Lesser said: all we have to do is care more and practice more than the other schools.

"The training rules? No, I don't see a problem for myself. I know Daddy would support it a hundred percent. What about you? How do you think you'll vote tomorrow? Right. Me, too. I'm all for it."

"Oh, I think most of the kids will vote for it. Sure. All of us would like to see Oregon City win *something* before we graduate. Arlene? Who knows? She not exactly the type to sacrifice anything, much less give up her Friday night dates for rehearsals."

It was not unusual for Julie's telephone visits with Carole to go on for a full hour. But tonight Julie's thoughts were elsewhere, and she moved to end the conversation early.

"Well, I've got some things to do still. Gotta run. I'll see you tomorrow in band. Right, Carole. See you tomorrow before school."

The interruption ended, Julie now could get to the "project" which she had assigned herself. Beneath the heading "NUMBER FOUR" she wrote:

    Three inches taller than me
    Handsome
    Nice build
    Good grades, rarely misses school
    Terribly shy
    No telephone number in the phone book
    Lives somewhere out Redland Road
    Miss Anderson told Mr. Cochran that No. 4 is one of the nicest boys
     she's ever had in her class
    Serious minded; never fools around in band
    Clothes, shoes must be from a poor family
    Turned Coach Shelton down on basketball and wrestling. Why?
    Turned Coach Ellis down on football and baseball. Why?
    Walks home alone after ball games. Why?

Julie spoke her thoughts out loud: "Not a bad list for a few days' research. Working in the office has its advantages. Now, let's see what we've got.

"On the plus side: He's tall enough; he's handsome; he's not going with anyone else; he's a senior; and he seems to be a really nice boy.

"On the other hand, he's the all-time shyest boy in Oregon; and he for sure doesn't have a car; and he doesn't seem to have a telephone; and he probably doesn't know how to dance.

"And he has gone into atomic paralysis anytime a girl has even looked at him. So why would it be any different with me? But what choice do I have? It's not as if there were a bunch of other tall guys to choose from.

Still, Number Four is *so* shy! she thought. For now I'd better keep this whole project hush-hush, and not tell even Carole yet. I guess maybe the first one to know should be Number Four himself.

Julie took another sheet of paper and began applying Miss Anderson's Principles of English Composition.

"Dear Andrew . . . ."

4
The Note

Tuesday, December 8; first period

The last students were arriving in the band room as Mr. Lesser emerged from the storage closet with a stack of music scores in his arms. In sharp contrast to yesterday's dark mood, there was an air of excitement and anticipation in the band room this Tuesday morning.

The tardy bell rang. Andrew put away his homework, and walked to his chair. As he opened the instrument case, he discovered a folded note inserted under the handle.

Never in seventeen years had Andrew received a note from a girl, and it simply did not cross his mind that this note might be from a girl. He removed the folded paper and quietly slipped it into his pocket, making sure that no one would notice. Then he assembled his saxophone.

Julie listened as Mr. Lesser talked and distributed music to the various section leaders. But Julie's eyes were on second chair tenor sax, anxious to see Andrew's reaction when he finally read her note.

Mr. Lesser returned to his place at the front of the band. "People, before we vote on yesterday's proposal, I want you to see the competition piece we'll be performing. I've chosen the Finale of Shostakovich's Fifth Symphony.

"Now, this is probably the most outstanding piece of music to come out of Russia in this century. As you look through it, you'll see that this is a very modern, very difficult piece, which also is very beautiful—after you get used to it. You'll find plenty of 32nd notes at *allegro*. It changes from 4/4 to 3/4 to 5/4 time, and so on. Some of you will be playing in four sharps, some in five. It is miserable in some places for clarinets and flutes, elsewhere for horns. In fact, *every* section will be challenged to the very limit. And that's why I selected this piece.

"That doesn't mean you can't do it. It's like I said yesterday: You can do *anything* if you are willing to pay the price. Now, how about it? Do you really *want* it?"

There was a long pause. "If you're willing to pay the price and abide by every one of the training rules," he continued as he pointed to the blackboard, "then stand up and be counted."

Many students, including Julie and Carole, Chuck and Wally, Arlene and others, stood immediately, then looked around, realizing how many still were seated. After some time, three more stood.

Andrew remained seated, his face deeply troubled, wanting to stand, but fearing his father's reaction. Julie was disappointed that Andrew was not already on his feet.

One boy stood, and started for the door. "Sir? I can't hack it. This is my senior year. Too many activities to pass up . . . basketball practice . . . I'm sorry, Sir."

"That's all right, Swenson. I'd rather know now than find out later. I'll transfer you to study hall."

"Me too, Sir." A girl started toward the door, and was joined by another girl.

"Yes. You, too, girls."

The standing students looked at each other, then at Mr. Lesser, then at those still seated. Then Wally spoke. "Hey, you creeps! Is this too much sacrifice for you? Are you shook up over a two hour sectional one night a week? Well, guess who's going to be here for two hours *every* night! That's right, Mr. Lesser will have to be here *every* night."

Several more students stood, a few at a time. But there were still a number of band members—Andrew included—who remained seated, still holding back.

Mr. Lesser spoke, quietly, almost in a whisper. "I forgot to mention one thing, People. We have a secret weapon."

"Sir?"

The band director's voice started quietly, then rose in intensity: "Me. I'm the secret weapon. I am quite simply the best high school band conductor in the State of Oregon—maybe in all of America. I'm good enough that I really ought to be conducting the New York Philharmonic. I know how to work and I know how to get teenagers to work. I demand perfection, and I get it. I'm a mean, rotten slave-driver of a band conductor. I can squeeze 100% out of any high school band. With you *wanting* to win, and with me *driving* you when the going gets tough, there is simply no risk. It's a sure thing. We *will* take State 4-A in band."

Chuck, already standing, jumped in. "That's right. We're going to take State *with* you guys or *without!* This is the last chance for you losers to be winners!"

With this, all of the remaining students, including Andrew, rose to their feet. The decision had been made: The Oregon City High School Concert Band had decided—had committed—to take State.

The bell rang, and Andrew hastily put his saxophone away. As the other students were leaving, he took the note from his pocket and quickly read it. A certain oboe player thought she saw a look of absolute astonishment on Andrew Sherwood's face.

The same day, after school

On the school bus Andrew usually kept pretty much to himself. So it did not seem strange to the other students this afternoon that Andrew sat alone with an open book on his lap, and that he gazed out the window at the rainy landscape.

What *was* unusual was what was going on inside Andrew's head. But then, no one could know that: A girl sent *me* a note? You've got to be kidding. Why would a girl write a note to some guy who is clumsy and ugly and wears the same pants every day and has cow manure on his shoes? Why would a girl ask a guy who can't dance to meet her at a sock hop?

Andrew read the note again.

> Dear Andrew—
>
> I think you and I are a lot alike, and maybe we are both lonely sometimes. I'll be looking for you at the sock hop in the gym Saturday afternoon.
>
> A Friend

Naw, there's something wrong here. Girls don't write notes to guys who are ugly and awkward and stupid. This must be some kind of set-up, some kind of joke. Maybe the punch line is when I make a complete fool of myself by showing up at the dance without a date. Or maybe the fun comes when whoever wrote this laughs at me in front of the whole school. Maybe the person who wrote this note is some guy trying to prove what a dolt I really am."

Making sure no one could see the paper, Andrew looked at the note again. Nice handwriting. Looks like a girl's writing, I guess. Jeez! What if this note is for real? What if there really is some girl who likes me? What if there really is some girl as lonely as I am?

If this is on the up and up, it must be some girl in the band. I mean, the note was in the handle of my saxophone case, right? But who? Who in the band would send me a note? Maybe I ought to go to the sock hop. You know, just look around. See if . . . ."

And then faint hope gave way to hard reality.

Right. You big dumb ox! First you say, "Pa, can I be excused from digging stumps and mending fences and chopping wood and cleaning out the barn today?"

And then Pa says, "Why, I'm sure we can work something out. What do you have in mind, Son?"

And then I say, "Well, Pa, it seems that some girl in the band has developed an interest in me."

Right. And then The Old Man smacks me with the back of his hand and laughs and laughs.

"*You?*" he says? "*You?* Some girl wants to dance with *you?* Why would a girl want to dance with a lazy, good-for-nothing, ugly loser?" And then he laughs and laughs and laughs, and we go back to rooting out stumps.

You bonehead! What makes you think you could go to a dance on a Saturday afternoon? What makes you think you could get a ride to town? What makes you think there really is a girl who likes you? What a joke."

Wednesday, December 9; first period [58 days to competition]

As soon as the bell rang, Mr. Lesser began an intense, driving hour of hard work with the members of the Oregon City High School Concert Band. "All right, People. Let's take it from the top. We'll keep the tempo slow until everyone can handle it at full speed."

Following the opening whole note *fortissimo* by the entire band, the brasses picked up the main theme of the *Finale* of Shostakovich's Fifth Symphony, accompanied by hammering eighth notes on the tympani. The whole band answered with four slashing eighth notes precisely on the beat. Then, the tempo accelerating, the flutes and clarinets picked up the theme and plunged into a blizzard of thirty-second notes imitating a howling wind right off the Steppes of Russia.

It sounded awful.

The leader of the New York Philharmonic brought the Oregon City High School Concert Band to a halt. "That part will need a lot of work," he said quietly. "All of it will need a lot of work."

"Flutes, clarinets, oboe this time. The rest of you follow along, reading your own parts. Let's take it from letter A. On the pickup note. Ready? And . . . ." The baton came down, signalling the high woodwinds. Mr. Lesser sang the main theme aloud, teaching, polishing, refining. Occasionally, he stopped to comment or to wipe perspiration from his face.

Then he led the brasses through their part. A trumpet man by trade, Ervin Lesser knew brasses inside and out, and could draw the best out of every trumpet, every trombone, every French horn. Skillfully he worked, explained, demonstrated, repeated.

While Mr. Lesser worked with the brasses, Julie watched Andrew. She thought she saw him shooting very brief glances at first one girl and then another—as though trying to solve some mystery. When he finally looked at her, Julie responded with a tiny smile, then looked away.

But there was no time for Julie's little project just now. Mr. Lesser was back to working with the entire band, and Julie had a difficult oboe part, often doubling with the flutes and clarinets on the main theme.

Only occasionally during the rest of the period was Julie able to sneak a glance at Andrew. But he didn't actually look at her again until the bell rang and everyone was putting away their instruments. Again, she gave him a small smile and looked away.

As he left the band room, Andrew Sherwood had a look of total amazement on his face.

Thursday, December 10; after school [57 days to competition]

After school, Andrew changed clothes and went to the woodpile near the barn. He threw a log on the sawhorse, and picked up the razor sharp cross-buck saw. Putting his left foot on the log, he began sawing the log, using the entire six foot length of his saw in long, expert strokes. In short order, Andrew had sawed through the log, and one more block of wood had been added to the pile at the end of the sawhorse.

Quickly, Andrew shifted the log on the sawhorse. Again he steadied the log with his left foot. Again he sawed off a block of wood. On the final cut, Andrew sawed the wood part way through, then picked up the log and cracked it sharply on the chopping block. Two more blocks of wood were added to the large pile.

Julie Ryckman, he thought. Julie Ryckman sends *me* a note?

More logs followed. For half an hour Andrew's arms and hands and left foot sawed wood while his mind grappled with the incomprehensible: A tall, very pretty, very nice *girl* had written him a note.

The sawing done, Andrew laid the saw aside and placed a block of wood on the chopping block. Quickly, he examined the block, found the knots, looked for cracks in the wood, and turned the block so that his axe would hit the exact place he had selected. Then Andrew brought the axe down sharply, and split the block into two pieces. With two more strokes, the two pieces became four blocks of fuel for the furnace in the basement. Every few seconds another block of wood became four pieces to be added to the pile.

The sawing and chopping finished, Andrew loaded a large stack of furnace wood on his left arm. He carried the load into the basement, and added it to the neat row of wood opposite the furnace. After several trips, the day's wood chopping was finished.

As he was leaving to feed the chickens, Andrew caught a reflection of himself in the basement window. He paused and considered his image in the glass. He pronounced the verdict aloud: "Too tall; ugly; clumsy; dumb; lazy; big hands; scared to death of girls." He believed every word of it.

"So what makes a nice girl like Julie Ryckman send *me* a note?" he thought aloud. "She's pretty, she gets good grades, everybody likes her . . . ."

Andrew went to the small chicken coop, where he filled the feed and water pans. From a large sack in the corner he took a quart of cracked grain, which he scattered on the ground for the twenty-nine hens. "Here you go, girls. You keep on producing eggs, and you keep on being hens. You slack off on the eggs and you'll be invited to Sunday dinner."

Then Andrew took the milk buckets and walked to the barn. "Who's first tonight?" he asked the two cows as they followed him into the barn. Daisy took her usual place on the left, Blossom on the right. Andrew broke open a bale of hay and scattered a quantity of fodder in the manger in front of each animal, then measured out some grain for them.

"Blossom," he started, "I asked Daisy what she thought about this note-writing business, but she didn't offer any suggestions. What do you think?" The warm milk made a pinging sound as it struck the bottom of the bucket.

"The question before the committee is simply this: why would Julie Ryckman, who is one of the prettiest girls around, invite *me* to meet her at the sock hop? I mean, she must know I don't have any nice clothes. She's probably noticed that I have only one pair of shoes. She must know I'm scared to death of girls. She may or may not know that I have no way to get to town on a Saturday—unless I hitch hike. She certainly knows that I'm ugly and stupid.

"So *why* does she invite me to meet her at the sock hop? Do you two ladies think she's setting me up for some kind of joke?"

Neither Daisy nor Blossom could provide any help with Andrew's questions. Andrew didn't bother asking the two cows whether they thought his father would let him go to town on a Saturday afternoon. He knew the answer to that question without asking.

Friday, December 11; lunch break [56 days to competition]

On Friday it happened again. When Andrew arrived in the band room with sack lunch in hand, he discovered a small folded note in the handle of his saxophone case. He was surprised not only to see the note, but to have proof that the first note had not been something he had imagined.

While everyone ate their lunches and listened to the record of the Fifth Symphony, Andrew quietly opened the note, making very sure no one would see, and read:

> Dear Andrew,
>
> I really mean it. I really will be at the sock hop tomorrow afternoon, and I really will be looking for you. Will you be there?
>
> Julie

Andrew guessed that Julie had been watching him, that she had known exactly when he had finished reading the note. He guessed that even now she was looking directly at him, and that if he looked toward her he would see two large brown eyes looking directly into his own eyes. And he knew that if he looked at her, she would give him a small smile and then look away. Andrew knew exactly what he would see if he looked at Julie.

Andrew looked. And he was right.

Sherwood, he thought to himself. You're a bonehead. You think she could do anything mean or cruel? With that smile? And those eyes? Not hardly, Dummy.

Friday afternoon

When the after-school rehearsal broke up, Andrew just stayed in the band room. There simply was no way to hitch hike home, have supper, do the chores, and be back by seven. Might as well stay here and do homework or practice.

As Julie left the band room, she saw that Andrew had made no move to put away his saxophone or to go home. It appeared that he was going to just stay in the band room until later when the others returned.

At the door she paused to look back at the tall tenor sax player who had now received two notes from her, and responded to neither with anything more than a glance and a blush.

The same evening

The members of the concert band were learning what Mr. Lesser had meant by hard work. Each day, every student had a rehearsal before school, another during first period, yet another during lunch, and one more rehearsal after school. Not to mention practicing at home and private lessons for many. Plus Mr. Lesser insisted that all homework for other teachers be kept current.

On Friday evening at seven, the members of the woodwind section had their turn with the sectional rehearsal routine. For two hard, driving hours Mr. Lesser led them through their parts, patiently tutoring them, demonstrating for them, teaching them, polishing the music.

At nine o'clock sharp the rehearsal ended. Julie had hoped that Andrew might linger after the practice, that he might say something about her notes or tomorrow's sock hop. Or, better yet, that he might invite her to go with him to the Burger Shack for a snack.

He didn't. Seemingly in a great rush, Andrew put his instrument away, pulled on his jacket, and walked out the door. Julie watched the tall boy, saxophone case in hand, hurrying down the hallway toward the street.

"Andrew Sherwood," she whispered, a puzzled look on her pretty face, "What's the hurry?"

She didn't know that Andrew had a seven mile walk ahead of him before he could do his chores or have supper. Nor could she know how important it was that Andrew arrive home before a certain man, who even now was sitting at a corner table at Coney Island Bar.

5
The Sock Hop

Saturday, December 12; afternoon [55 days to competition]

Julie had been to other sock hops, but this one, she hoped, was going to be special. At *this* sock hop she would be dancing—and with a boy three inches taller than she was!

Before lunch, Julie had gone to Audre's on Main Street to pick out a beautiful new skirt and sweater and matching shoes. Then she had gone to Esther's and had her hair done in the latest style—with curly bangs high on her forehead and soft curls turning up at her shoulders.

Time to get dressed for the dance. Alone in her bedroom, Julie picked up the framed photograph of her now deceased mother. A wave of—what was it? loneliness? sadness? closed in on Julie. She missed her mother more than ever before.

Looking into her mirror, Julie saw how much she resembled the slim young woman in the portrait. Mom would know which perfume to use, which lipstick would be best with this outfit. Mom would have helped her get ready, would have fussed over her and told her how beautiful she was.

But Mom was in a grave in Michigan. Julie would have to do the best she could alone.

Julie had pulled on the new sweater and saw again how nice it looked with the wool skirt flaring wide and reaching to below her knees.

Then she had added hopefully just the right touch of eye makeup and hopefully just the right lipstick plus one dab of perfume behind each ear. "Just right," she said. "I hope."

"Julie, Dear," she said to her image in the mirror, "you look simply stunning. Poor Andrew won't have a chance once he sees you in this outfit." Her brave words belied the insecurity she felt.

Julie clipped a tiny earring to each ear. Then she added the final touch—the ultimate luxury which she had been saving for last—on her feet she slipped her first-ever pair of not-very-high heels.

Speaking again to the beautiful young woman in the mirror, Julie said, "I predict that for your first real date, Andrew will take you to the Christmas Ball." A small shiver of anticipation ran through her.

"Julie!" Carole exclaimed when Julie arrived to pick her up, "What a beautiful outfit! And heels! You are an absolute smash!

"Don't tell me! Let me guess! Some boy has asked you to meet him at the sock hop! Who is he? Is he handsome? Is he a senior? Does he go to Oregon City High? Do I know him?" Carole's questions had tumbled out in an unanswerable confusion.

"You goose," Julie had answered. "No one has asked me to meet him at the sock hop. Promise. Is it such a big deal that I buy something pretty to wear once in a while?"

"You don't fool me for one minute, Julie Ryckman," Carole had laughed. "We've been to a lot of sock hops together, and you've never yet worn heels until today! I think you'd better tell me all about this."

"We shall see what we shall see" was all Julie would say as she parked her father's car in the student parking lot.

Sock hops were invented specifically for the benefit and convenience of unattached high school students. Boys without girlfriends came to look at the girls, without wanting it to appear that· they were looking at the girls. Girls without boyfriends came to be seen, without wanting it to seem that they were there to be seen.

Entering the gym, the two girls observed that the universal rules regulating sock hops were in full force: all the boys were standing against the east wall of the gym, and all the girls against the west. As usual, the boys were clustered in little groups with their buddies, talking about the girls and daring one another to ask some girl to dance.

As usual, the girls were standing in small groups with their friends, talking about the boys and hoping some boy would ask them to dance.

For boys, the customary dress at a sock hop was pretty informal, except for socks. (At a sock hop it was considered poor form to wear smelly old socks with holes in them.) On the other hand, girls tended to put a lot of time into hairdos and dresses and makeup.

Music at a sock hop was provided by a record player and one large speaker. The 45-rpm records featured the latest ballads, plus music of the Big Band era—mostly fox-trots, jitterbugs, boogie-woogies, and an occasional waltz.

It took only a moment for Julie to determine that Andrew Sherwood was not among the boys in the room. At six-foot-three, he tended to stand out in any group. Not here yet, she thought to herself. But he'll come. I know he'll come.

A half hour passed. Carole danced a waltz with one boy, and a jitterbug with another. For all her expense and preparation and hopes, the tallest girl in school—now even taller in her new heels—simply stood and waited.

"He's shy," she reasoned. "But he'll come. He got my notes—and he looked at me and he saw me smile at him. I know he'll come . . . ."

An hour later, the dance ended. Julie tried very hard not to show Carole and the other girls how terribly hurt and disappointed she was. Struggling to maintain her composure as she drove, Julie dropped Carole off and drove home.

Alone in the house, Julie entered her bedroom and abandoned her brave composure. Great weeping sobs racked her as she put a record on her phonograph, then lifted the return arm so the same record would play over and over and over. As the soft, sad music played, Julie took off her dress and shoes and put them away.

> They're writing songs of love—but not for me.
> A lucky star's above—but not for me.
> With love to lead the way, I found more skies of gray
> Than any Russian play could guarantee . . . .
> Although I can't dismiss the memory of his kiss,
> I guess he's not for me.

If the day's disappointments hadn't been enough to bring Julie Ryckman to a genuine crying jag, the music was. As she cried herself to sleep, the song repeated the bitter words again and again:

> "I guess he's not for me . . . ."

Saturday evening

It had been a long day for Alton Ryckman, and he was happy to be closing up the office. He said good-night to the cleaning lady, put a folded copy of this week's newly-printed *Oregon City Enterprise* in his coat pocket and left for home.

Remembering that Julie had borrowed the car, Mr. Ryckman walked up the stone steps which led from lower Oregon City, where the *Enterprise* offices were located, to upper Oregon City, where the small but neat Ryckman home was situated. As he climbed the 215 steps, he marvelled again that the Founding Fathers had seen fit to establish a city with a ninety-foot cliff between the two halves of town.

"Must have been exercise nuts, those pioneers," he mused aloud. "Probably all lived to be a hundred years old, what with all the stair-climbing they had to do . . . ."

Arriving at a landing part way up the stairs, Mr. Ryckman paused to look once again at his city—his Oregon City. There at his feet was the lower part of the town, huddled in a narrow strip between the cliff and the river. In that part of town were located the older shops, stores, and office buildings. In the 1800s this had been the whole of the town, until lack of room forced the city fathers to expand to the only available space, 90 feet straight up.

To his left were the historic Willamette Falls, where the Clackamas Indians once speared salmon, and where now two giant factories worked around the clock making paper for Crown-Zellerbach.

Across the river he could see West Linn. To his daughter and her high school friends, West Linn was "The Enemy." To him, it was just another part of an extended community of suburbs ringing the southern fringe of Portland—a ring of potential advertisers and customers for his *Oregon City Enterprise*.

Spanning the river and connecting Oregon City with West Linn stood an ancient two-lane bridge. The roadbed was supported by four bridge towers and twin arching spans. Far below the bridge the dark, cold waters of the Willamette flowed north toward Portland and the mighty Columbia River.

Behind and above him was upper Oregon City, the location of most of the town's homes, churches and schools. Even after living in Oregon City for nearly four years, Alton Ryckman found it strange that so many people could live above a cliff and work below it.

By now there was, of course, the beautiful new elevator which the city's leaders had constructed to replace the former creaking turn-of-the-century elevator. Alton took pride in the role his newspaper had played in that vital project. Today, people could go from lower to upper Oregon City and back in total comfort and convenience—and at no cost—on the beautiful new municipal elevator.

Convenience and comfort were one thing, but editors who sit at desks needed exercise, too. Alton preferred to use the ancient stone stairs, especially when Julie had the car.

Thinking of his daughter—she'd likely have dinner ready about now. Alton Ryckman quickened his pace toward home and a hot meal.

When he got home, Mr. Ryckman found the house dark, yet the car was in the driveway. Concerned, he entered the house and turned on a light. No Julie in sight, no pleasant dinner smells from the kitchen, no cheerful welcome home.

He walked down the hall toward Julie's room, and heard music coming from inside. He knocked gently on the door, waited a moment, then turned the handle.

There on the bed, fast asleep and looking fragile, lay the tall, slender daughter who filled Alton Ryckman's life with joy and hope—the beautiful daughter who looked so much like the girl Alton had courted and married and loved . . . and lost.

He stepped to the phonograph and listened to the record, which had been playing for two hours now:

> They're writing songs of love—but not for me.
> A lucky star's above—but not for me . . . .

He lifted the needle from the disc and switched the record player off.

The sudden stillness awakened the girl. "Daddy?" She turned to face the man she loved so much.

"Honey, what is it? Why, you've been crying?"

"It's . . . it's all right, Daddy . . . I'm fine . . . ."

"You're not fine. What is it, Sis? Can I help?"

"Oh, Daddy, it's . . . it's just one of those . . . . Oh, it's nothing, really. I guess I'm a silly goose." Suddenly aware of the time, and wanting to change the subject, Julie exclaimed, "Oh, and it's dinner time and I haven't done a thing! I haven't even done the grocery shopping yet."

"Tell you what, Sis. You wash your pretty face and put on something nice. I'm taking you out to dinner tonight."

"Oh, but I've let you down . . . ."

"Tut, tut. I won't hear a word of it. I've asked you out, and I won't take 'no' for an answer. Now hustle your bustle: I'm starving, and I'll bet you are, too."

As Julie finished her dinner at Chicken-in-a-Basket, her father took her hand and said, "Sis, who loves you?"

"My Daddy."

"Do you really believe that?"

"I really believe that."

"And who would rather hurt in a hundred places than have you hurt in one place?"

"My Daddy."

"Do you really believe that?"

"I really believe that."

"And who can help you when you've got a problem and it looks like there's no solution?"

"My Daddy."

"Do you really believe that?"

"I really believe that."

There was a pause as both father and daughter thought of what each had just said—and knew that it was absolutely true.

"Something happened today that made my girl cry herself to sleep while listening to sad music. When you're ready to have me kiss it and make it better, you'll let me know? . . . ."

"Oh, Daddy . . . since Mom died, you've been mother and father and best friend to me. I don't know what I'd have done without you . . . . But I'm not sure that any man—even my own dear Daddy—can help me with this."

"That bad, huh, Sis?"

"That bad. Daddy, I'm six feet tall, and . . . ."

He interrupted. "Five-foot-twelve."

Julie laughed. "Yes. Five-foot-twelve, which is almost as bad as six feet even. But, Daddy, I'm so tall, taller than most of the boys . . . and I'm a senior and I'm seventeen, and I see all my friends going out on dates and wearing pretty dresses to dances and having boyfriends, and I . . . ."

"And you haven't ever had a date."

"Yes."

"And you worry that you'll finish high school, and never have had a date."

"Yes."

"And you worry that you'll never find Prince Charming and that you'll be an old maid . . . ."

"Yes. That, too."

"Anything else?"

"Well, there is this one boy . . . ."

"And you kind of like him?"

"I think I like him. I'm not sure if I like him, or if he's just the only **tall** boy left for me . . . ."

"And he likes you?"

"I don't know. I thought maybe he would come to the sock hop today . . . ."

"But he didn't come."

"He didn't come. I had on a pretty outfit, and I had my hair done, and I even wore a pair of heels. But he . . . he didn't come."

"And you think he doesn't care for you."

"I don't know what to think. I sent him a couple of notes. I told him I'd be looking for him at the sock hop. I really thought he'd come. But I guess he doesn't like me . . . ."

"Maybe you are getting to the conclusion before you have all your facts. Tell me, what do you know about him?"

"Well . . . he's tall—three inches taller than I am . . . ."

"Five-foot-fifteen?"

Julie laughed again. "Yes, five-foot-fifteen. And he lives out in the country somewhere—out Redland Road, I think. His folks don't seem to have a telephone. And he's in the band. He's really good on the tenor sax . . . ."

"You haven't mentioned the important things."

"Well, he gets good grades. He's polite . . . very quiet. I think maybe he's the shyest person I've ever met. He seems very nice . . . ."

"Sounds like a nice boy. Does this tall tenor sax player have a name?"

"Andrew. Andrew Sherwood."

"Know what I think, Sis? If your Andrew Sherwood is as shy as you say he is, he'd have a hard time showing up at a sock hop, even to dance with Julie Ryckman. Or, if he lives way out in the country, as you say, maybe he just had no way to get to town for the sock hop. Or maybe he has a job Saturdays. Or . . . something.

"My guess is that come Monday morning Andrew will meet you at school and apologize for not being there, and all your tears will have been for nothing. You'll see."

Sunday, December 13; evening *[54 days to competition]*

Andrew Sherwood was alone in his bedroom, sitting on the bed and trying to write a note to Julie. Next to him were several crumpled papers, evidence of how hard this project was, and of how little progress he was making. He started again:

> Dear Julie—
> I'm sorry I couldn't come to the sock hop. My dad had me working until late evening, and I

"Naw. That's no good." Another crumpled paper was added to the pile.

> Dear Julie—
> I really tried to get up the courage to ask my Dad if I could

"Naw. That's no good either. She wouldn't understand." Yet another wad of paper went onto the pile.

> Dear Julie—
> I wish we had a telephone so I could have called you and told you why I couldn't

"Rats." Crumpled paper.

> Dear Julie—
> I didn't come to the sock hop because I only have one pair of shoes, and they had gotten all wet and muddy while I was digging a stump out of the pasture, and I

Crumpled paper.

In his mind Andrew could picture Miss Anderson telling her English students how they should not begin writing until they had decided exactly what they wanted to say.

"Good idea," he said out loud. Then Andrew began writing exactly what he wanted to say.

> Dear Julie—
>
> I can't tell you how flattered I was that a beautiful and popular girl like you would write me a note, and invite me to meet you at the sock hop. I don't know what you see in someone as ugly and awkward and dumb as I am, but I'm happier than I've ever been that you seem to care.
>
> I wanted so badly to meet you at the sock hop, but my Dad works me pretty hard, especially on Saturdays, so I couldn't get away. Besides, I don't have any clothes or shoes I could wear to a sock hop, nor any way to get there unless I got lucky hitch hiking. Plus, my Dad drinks quite a bit, so there's no money for me to buy you a soda or a present.
>
> Anyway, I guess I wouldn't know what to say to you. I couldn't tell you what I really think—that I think you're pretty and that I like you a lot.
>
> Thanks for caring and for writing, Julie. I wish there were some way this could work out between us, but I know it can't. You're much too good for a big, dumb farm boy anyway.
>
> Andrew.

Monday, December 14 [53 days to competition]

On the way to school Andrew read his note—his letter—to Julie several times, making sure that no one on the bus could see what he had written.

He had planned to give the note to Julie as soon as he saw her, but then she entered the band room with Carole, and he decided to wait. He noticed that she did look at him, but that something had changed. Instead of glancing at him and then turning away with a smile, she just looked straight at him, as though asking a question with her eyes: "Why, Andrew? Why didn't you come? Don't you have something you want to tell me?"

But then the rehearsal began, and Andrew had no opportunity to talk with Julie.

"After first period band," he said to himself. "I'll wait until everyone has left the band room, then slip the note to Julie. Right after first period, for sure."

But when first period ended, there arose such a thumping in Andrew's chest, and such a fear of actually standing face to face with Julie, and talking with her, that he simply could not do it.

All through English Andrew worked up his courage. All through algebra he vowed to give Julie the note at the beginning of the lunchtime rehearsal. All through his gym class he thought of what he might say, what she might say. "Lunch time," he said to himself. "Lunch time, do or die."

To get to his saxophone, Andrew had to walk through a doorway into the band's storage room. He was terrified to discover that Julie was standing directly in the doorway and that there was no one near them.

Andrew nearly fainted with fear. His heart pounded, and his legs seemed unable to support his weight. All the blood in his body seemed to rush to his head.

Very quietly, Julie said, "Hello, Andrew." That was all.

"I . . . ah . . . I . . . . I mean . . . ." Andrew was unable to say anything more. An eternity of silence passed as the shyest person in the Northern Hemisphere tried to speak.

"Julie, I . . . . Julie, you . . . ." Silence once more. Andrew reached in his pocket and started to remove the note he had written.

And then, sack lunches in hand, several other band members arrived. Andrew put the note back in his pocket, and mumbled something about having to get his saxophone case.

The lunch-time rehearsal went well, though looking back at it later, Andrew Sherwood could only recall his terror at the thought that sooner or later he would have to stand close to this pretty girl and finish what he had started to say.

All through Miss Perry's American History class Andrew thought of how he might say what he had to say without saying it. All through Mr. Goodmanson's physics class he worked up his courage, vowing that he would talk to Julie at the end of the after-school rehearsal, after the other band members had left.

At letter "J" in the Fifth Symphony, Dmitri Shostakovich created an incredibly beautiful passage featuring moody whole notes in the horns, offset by a hypnotizing counterpoint of quarter notes played by the flutes and clarinets. The entire passage is played pianissimo—very softly—and ends in barely audible echoes of the flute-clarinet melody played on a xylophone.

During the after-school polishing of this passage, players of tenor saxes and oboes spend a lot of time counting bars and waiting their turn to play. Sometimes, during such polishing, oboe players may smile shyly at tenor sax players, as if to say "I want to give you the benefit of the doubt. I want to make it as easy as possible for you to say something to me. I hope you'll let me see the note you almost gave me."

And sometimes, while flutes and clarinets and horns and xylophones slave over a beautiful passage, tenor sax players may sneak quick glances at pretty oboe players, and work up their courage and promise themselves that this time . . . this time . . . .

The hour ended. "People, are you beginning to enjoy Shostakovich?" Mr. Lesser asked. "Have you ever heard anything more beautiful than what we've just practiced?

"Now trumpets, cornets, don't forget our sectional tonight at seven. Dismissed."

Except for a tenor sax player and an oboist, the band members quickly put their instruments away and hurried out of the band room. Julie lingered just outside the band room door—the door through which, sooner or later, Andrew would have to pass.

"Hi." Julie spoke in a whisper.

"Hi. It's . . . It's . . . I like the music." There. A whole sentence.

Julie knew she was speaking to a frightened deer in the forest. She kept · her voice very low, and was careful not to assault Andrew with a direct gaze at his face. "Yes. I thought the Fifth was awful when we first started playing it, but now I'm starting to enjoy it." Julie chanced a quick glance at Andrew, and showed him her warmest smile. "Sometimes I catch myself humming The Fifth at home."

"Yes."

"Andrew, I . . . I was sorry you couldn't get to the sock hop."

"I . . . I . . . ah . . . ." The panic was returning. The red face, the pounding heart, the icy fear. "Julie, I . . . Well, I . . . ." Andrew looked at his shoes and saw how bad they looked. "I guess I . . . ."

There was no mistaking the terror in Andrew's eyes and voice. "It's all right, Andrew. It's all right. Is there something you want to tell me?"
"Yes."
"But it's hard to talk sometimes?"
"Yes."
There was a long pause. "Julie? I . . . ah . . . I've . . . I've got to go. I . . . I have to . . . ."
Julie touched Andrew's arm, and she saw the panic in his eyes. Her deer was about to flee to the forest.
"It's all right, Andrew. Andrew? Please . . . Don't be afraid of me. I'll never hurt you. I promise. You have nothing to fear from me. I want for us to be friends."
Andrew, still unable to speak, nodded that he understood.
"I'll see you tomorrow," Julie said gently. Without further word, Andrew picked up his tenor sax case and escaped.
As he strode down the steep hill on Washington Street, Andrew once more read the note he had prepared for Julie. He stopped beside Tony's Fish Market for a long time, deep in thought. Then he threw the note into a trash can, and began walking toward Redland Road.
Andrew would surely have died had he known that someone else had seen all this. Sixty seconds after he threw it away, Andrew's discarded note to Julie was being read by another member of the band.

Tuesday, December 15; before school [52 days to competition]

Early Tuesday morning Julie arrived at school and walked to her locker. As usual, Carole was there waiting for her. Julie opened her locker, and was about to put her books inside when she saw what looked like a note. Apparently, someone had slipped the note into the locker through one of the ventilating slots near the top of the locker door.
Hoping Carole hadn't seen the folded note, Julie put her books inside the locker, deftly palmed the note, and closed the door. The two girls, instrument cases in hand, walked toward the band room.
After a time Carole asked The Question: "Julie? Are we best friends?"
"Of course."
"And don't best friends tell each other everything?"
"Of course."

"Then what's with the heels at the sock hop? And what's with the note you're hiding in your right hand?"

Same day; evening

Finishing his dinner, Alton Ryckman wiped his mouth with his napkin and pushed his chair back from the table.

"Good chow in this mess hall, Sarge," he said to Julie. "But if you're going to feed me this well, I'm going to have to climb the stairs ten times a day."

Julie smiled. It pleased her that her father noticed the good things she did and that he took time to compliment her. It was not easy doing all the housework, all the shopping, all the cooking. Julie had struggled at first, until she had learned that the washer and the dryer can run at the same time as the oven and the mixer.

With all her responsibilities at home, and with all her class work plus band rehearsals and oboe practice at home, Julie had to make each moment count, especially if she were to have any kind of social life.

"Well, Sis, how's Andrew? Last I heard he had stood up the prettiest girl at Oregon City High for a sock hop, and she had decided he didn't like her."

"He likes me." There was just a trace of smug satisfaction in Julie's smile.

"He likes you?"

"He likes me." There it was again.

Alton Ryckman was enjoying Julie's little game. "Apparently you have some reason to think so."

"Correct."

"Such as . . . ."

"He put a note in my locker today."

"And he said . . . ?"

"He said, 'I think I like you.'"

"Let me see: 'I—think—I—like—you'. Five words. He's not one to multiply words, is he?"

"Daddy, I'd guess that putting those five words on paper and then putting the note in my locker may have been one of the most difficult things Andrew Sherwood ever did."

"Pretty shy, huh?"

"Desperately shy. I've never known a person who had such fear of people. I don't know why he's so afraid, but he nearly fainted yesterday when I tried to talk to him."

"Did he manage to say anything?"

"Not much. He'd like to say something, I'm sure of it. But it is so terribly hard for him."

"Julie, it sounds like this young man really needs help—really needs a friend. I think maybe you've found yourself a project."

"I know. I started out just hoping for something for myself—a boyfriend and some dates. But I feel like this is changing, like maybe I need to do something to help poor Andrew."

"I agree, Sis. You can probably do more for Andrew right now than anyone else. With your kindness and compassion, you've got the right tools."

Julie smiled. "There is one more tool I could really use."

"Hmmm?"

"A formal dress. Daddy, I think I'll need a formal dress for the Christmas Ball."

Alton Ryckman laughed. "I'll put in a good word with Santa Claus."

Wednesday, December 16; late evening [51 days to competition]
Andrew had finished his other chores and was milking the cows when the lights of his father's pickup appeared in the driveway.

Seeing the dim light of the flashlight in the barn, Jim opened the gate to the pasture and walked unsteadily toward the barn. Andrew could smell the alcohol on his father's breath.

Andrew's father found a second milk stool and sat down next to his boy. "Evenin', Son."

"Evening, Pa."

Jim's voice was slurred by the beer he had drunk, but there was a gentleness in the older man's voice. "'Bout got 'er done up, Son?"

"Daisy's done. I won't be long with Blossom."

"Well, Son, how's the music comin'?"

"Fine, Pa. It's coming along just fine."

"Good. A boy needs to feel like he's good at somethin' . . . . Well, a *father* needs to feel like *he's* good at somethin'."

"No trouble, there, Pa. There's nobody around who can work like you do."

"That's right! My step-dad made sure of that! He'd leave a list of jobs for me in the mornin', and if I ever came up short, he'd . . . ."

Andrew waited, knowing his father wouldn't finish the sentence this time any more than he had on a hundred other occasions. Finally, Andrew changed subjects.

"Pa? You got a lot of music in you. I mean, nobody sings nicer than you do . . . . Were you ever in the band or the chorus or anything like that . . . when you were in high school, I mean?"

"No time, I reckon. My step-dad wouldn't put up with that. He figured things like band and football and all such was a waste of time and tax money. *'Work!'*, he said. 'You got to learn to *work!* School ain't for fun and games, but to get you ready for a world of work!' Then the Depression came along, and I learned he was right. Only those who knew how to work could keep a job."

"Yes, Pa . . . and I'm trying to learn to work hard, too."

"Right! Ain't no boy in the county can outwork my boy!"

Andrew took quiet pride in the knowledge that what his father had just said was probably true. "Pa? Did you ever have a girlfriend when you were in high school?"

"I did, once. A real nice girl, she was. That was before I met your Ma, mind you."

"Did you ever go to dances or ball games with her?"

"No. My step-dad wouldn't let me. 'Time enough for foolin' around with girls after you learn to work and can support a wife and family,' he said."

"Yeah. I suppose so. Still, sometimes a girl looks at me and smiles and I get all red in the face and I can't talk straight, and . . . ."

"I know. That's how I felt when I first started courtin' your Ma. She was somethin', I'll tell you . . . ."

"She still is, Pa. And she loves you, too."

"Lord knows why! I leave her waitin' for me nights while I'm soppin' up beer at Coney Island, and her here all alone. It ain't right. No sir, she deserves better."

By now Andrew had finished the milking. He carried both buckets while steadying his father as they walked to the house. Andrew left the buckets on the porch, then helped his father to the bedroom. Gently,

Andrew eased his father's boots off, then covered the older man with a blanket.

"Fine boy," murmured Jim Sherwood. "Fine boy. That's a boy a man can be proud of . . . ." Andrew turned off the bedroom light and quietly closed the door. His mother was there to embrace him.

"Ma? He's so gentle sometimes when he's drunk. Sometimes when he's drunk, we talk—just like we were friends. Why can't Pa talk nice to me when he's sober?"

Alice Sherwood looked at Andrew, then gave a tiny shrug of her shoulders. Swallowing her tears, she held her boy close.

6
The Fence

Thursday, December 17; evening [*50 days to competition*]

Andrew had to walk for nearly two miles before he got a ride. Then he had to walk the remaining one mile down Ferguson Road before he could begin his chores, his homework, and his hours of saxophone practice and homework. He was getting a late start.

"Bad news, Son. The cows got out." Andrew's mother was sincerely sorry for the extra work she was announcing to a son whom she considered to be already overworked. "Mr. Copley saw them wandering down the road, and he tied them up. You'll need to go get them."

"Dumb cows . . . . Yeah, Ma. I'll go get 'em." Andrew put on his jacket and started the half-mile hike down the hill to the Copley place on Abernathy Creek.

"That's just what I need," Andrew grumbled to himself. "I didn't have enough to do tonight without those dumb cows breaking through the fence and playing tourist. Won't get to bed 'til midnight at this rate."

After Andrew had thanked old Mr. Copley for rounding up the two stray cows, he untied them and turned them up the road toward home. He stayed just behind the animals with a switch in hand—a switch more for appearances than anything else, for the cows knew the way home, and were tired of their great adventure. What they wanted most was to have their hay and grain and to be milked.

But the road led uphill, and the way was steep. It took quite a while before the cows were in their barn and the milking could be done.

Then, working by flashlight, Andrew found the break in the fence and hastily repaired it. "That will have to do until Saturday," he said to himself. "Hope those two dumb cows can leave this alone until I have time to do the job right . . . ."

Then it was back to the normal after-school routine—only a couple of hours behind schedule: saw firewood; chop firewood; move firewood to the basement; feed and water the chickens; gather the eggs; strain the milk;

put the milk in gallon bottles for Ma to sell; take off the jacket; leave the shoes on the enclosed porch; go in the house and wash up; eat supper with Ma; do homework; practice the saxophone for two hours; collapse exhausted into bed.

But before turning off the light, Andrew read Julie's most recent note once more.

> Dear Andrew—
>
> I was *delighted* to receive your note. I know it's hard for you to talk with me, so I'll be happy just to get notes from you until you feel ready to talk.
>
> Would it would be easier for you to talk on the telephone? I'd love to have you call me.
>
> Love, Julie

Friday, December 18; evening *[49 days to competition]*

It was getting harder for Julie to keep her "romance" with Andrew quiet. Carole kept pressing Julie for the "inside skinny," to which her best-friend status entitled her. And how long could Julie and Andrew keep exchanging shy (his) and sly (hers) smiles in band before someone guessed what was happening?

Julie sensed how vital it was that word not get around yet. Andrew was so desperately shy! If he thought others were talking about him—linking his name with that of a girl, he would just die. No, better to keep this thing very quiet for now.

Besides, if everything went according to plan, everyone would find out soon enough—when Julie made her grand entry at the Christmas Ball on Andrew Sherwood's arm.

When the Friday night woodwind sectional broke up, Julie waited until everyone else had left the band room, then casually walked past her tall saxophone player and said, "Good-night, Andrew." Quietly, she slipped a note and a picture of herself into his saxophone case, and then left. She knew it would be easier for Andrew if she were not there when he read her note and what she had written on the photograph.

Julie had not walked more than ten steps when she heard Andrew's voice behind her, calling her.

"Julie? Thank you for the picture. And . . . the answer is, yes."

Julie turned and stared at Andrew. His voice had been perfectly calm, perfectly confident. He was looking directly into her eyes as he said, " Yes, Julie. I'd like to take you to the Christmas Ball."

Saturday, December 19; morning [48 days to competition]

Andrew was in the pasture with his father, digging out yet another huge stump, when Mr. Copley's old truck pulled into the Sherwood driveway. Instinctively, Andrew looked for Daisy and Blossom and saw neither of them.

Andrew's father told the boy to continue working, and walked over to greet his neighbor. Though he tried, Andrew could not hear what the two men were saying, but in his heart he knew: the cows must have gotten out again.

When finally Mr. Copley left, Andrew's father returned to his son with blood in his eyes. "It's the cows," he said in a very cold, controlled voice. "Twice in a week the cows are out through the fence and wandering down the road. Twice in a week Mr. Copley leaves his work to go round up our cows. I guess Mr. Copley ain't got enough to do without herding our cows?"

As he spoke, Jim Sherwood warmed to his subject. Gradually, his voice became louder, until at the end he was shouting. "Now if the cows get out once, a smart person knows there's a problem with the fence, and he takes care of it. Only a lazy jackass leaves the problem so the cows can get out again, right? A smart person knows that cows wandering on country roads get hit by cars, right? And that the cars that hit them get wrecked, right?

"So, what does that make you? Either you are a stupid, lazy idiot, or you want to see the cows dead and your Old Man sued out of his socks. Either way, you're dumber than the law allows!

"Now get your lazy butt down to Copleys' and bring those stupid cows home! And when you get back here, I will have a little job waiting for you—something to help you remember to fix the stupid fence right the *first* time you see a problem!"

It was a Saturday Andrew would never forget. After he had brought the cows home and tied them up, Andrew's jury had found him guilty, and his judge had pronounced the sentence: "You, my idiot son, are going to build a new fence around the pasture!"

Andrew was stunned by the severity of the sentence. "Pa . . . the whole pasture?"

"Yes, Idiot, the whole blasted three acres, and done right! I want all new fence posts, and I want them in holes thirty inches deep. I want fence posts absolutely in a straight line. And yes, Idiot, I want them all the way around the pasture!"

"Pa . . . . I messed up— not fixing the fence right the other night. But it was late, and I had so much to do . . . ."

"You had so much to do," the older man mocked. "But you had two hours to fool with that saxophone, making that damnable racket! That's what you had to do. Well, you are going to do something useful just once, you lazy idiot! You are going to build a fence, and you are going to do it right!"

"Where we going to get that many fence posts, Pa?"

"*You* are going to *make* them, with a saw and an axe and a wedge and a sledge hammer."

"Pa, I . . . ."

"Shut your stupid mouth! I'm tired of your lame excuses. Now help me root this stump out of the ground."

"Pa? . . . . If we're going to root out stumps all day today, when am I going to put in the new fence?"

"Good question, Donderhead. Maybe you should have thought of that when you did half a job fixing the fence the other night."

Sunday, December 20 *[47 days to competition]*

Usually, Andrew had Sunday as a day of rest, with only morning and evening chores to do. But today he had no choice but to work, and to work hard. He arose before daybreak to get an early start on his milking and other chores, and then turned his attention to building the new fence.

"One thing I *know*," he said as he pulled on his jacket. "Any talk of going to the Christmas Ball with Julie is out the window unless that new fence is finished. And the Christmas Ball is Wednesday night . . . ."

Three acres of pasture-land to fence. Andrew estimated that he would need close to 250 posts—and 250 post-holes. There was simply no way on God's green earth that a boy could pull it off by Wednesday night. But Andrew knew he *had* to pull it off.

In the forest he looked for a good, straight fir tree of perhaps sixteen-inches diameter at the butt. Using his cross-buck saw, he made his first cut some six inches above the ground. A few skillful swings of the axe removed the wood above the cut, leaving a "V." Then he made a second cut a few inches higher than the first on the back side of the tree. As soon as the saw was entirely within the wood, he hammered a steel wedge in behind it to prevent the weight of the tree from binding on the saw. Then he alternately cut with the saw and hammered on the wedge until the tree fell with a crash in the forest.

Then, axe in hand, he went down the entire length of the tree, each swing removing a limb exactly at the trunk of the tree, leaving only a small indentation to show where the limb had been.

Next, using the cross-buck saw, he cut the trunk of the tree into eight-foot lengths. Finally, he employed the steel wedges and fourteen-pound hammer and axe to split each eight-foot log into fence posts.

As he worked, Andrew thought of what he had committed himself to last Friday night. He had made a promise, had given Julie his word that he would take her to the Christmas Ball.

Resting for a moment, Andrew took the photograph of Julie from his pocket and held it close to his face so he could make out the faint scent of her perfume. Then he considered the girl in the picture, her pretty face, her warm smile, her hair done just so for her class picture. And the inscription, "Love, Julie," written in the corner.

Andrew turned the picture over and read once more the words he knew from memory. "Each time you look at this picture, I'll be thinking of you."

Andrew had promised to take Julie to the Christmas Ball. It was unthinkable to go back on his word—unthinkable to disappoint her again. And besides that, he *wanted* more than anything else in life to go with her. Andrew returned Julie's picture to his shirt pocket and went back to work.

"But *how* do I take Julie to the dance?" he said aloud. "There is flat no way the Old Man will let me go to the dance if this fence isn't finished first."

By mid-afternoon Andrew had turned three trees into fence posts. Carrying the posts two at a time on his shoulder, the tall boy brought the fence posts to the pasture, and dropped them one at a time about every six feet around the perimeter of the pasture.

"Not nearly enough," he said to himself. "Going to have to cut up a lot more trees to get enough posts . . . ."

A thought made its way to Andrew's lips—half soliloquy and half prayer: "Dear God in heaven, please help me to get through this. It's less than four days until the Christmas Ball, and I've got all this fence to build, and I've got homework and rehearsing and walking home from school." Andrew returned to his task, working even faster than before.

Beginning at the barn, Andrew strode to the corner of the pasture, where he drove a stake in the ground. To this he tied a heavy piece of twine which he stretched taut back to the barn. Now he could be sure his post holes would be in a straight line.

Most of the post holes were easy to dig. But where there were stones or tree roots, the process was difficult. First, Andrew used the tape measure to be sure each post was exactly six feet from the last. Then he used the shovel to dig out a round piece of sod. Taking the post hole tool with one wooden handle in each hand, Andrew brought the tool down hard on the ground. Twin shovel-like blades sliced into the dirt. Then he pulled the handles apart, forcing the blades below the pivot to close on the dirt between. Up out of the hole Andrew lifted a quantity of dirt.

As the process was repeated again and again, the tool bit deeper and deeper into the earth until a post-hole thirty inches deep had been formed. Then into the hole went one of the newly split posts. Using the spirit level to make sure the post was exactly plumb, and the string to be sure it was exactly in line, Andrew filled in around the post with dirt and rocks. Finally, turning the shovel upside down, he tamped the dirt in firmly around the new post. Later, when all the posts were in, he would tie up the cows and transfer the three strands of barbed wire from the tired old fence posts to the beautiful, straight, new posts.

Only twice during the day did Andrew stop, and then only briefly. At mid-day his mother brought him some lunch, and in the evening he gulped down some dinner before doing his chores.

Andrew was vaguely aware throughout the day that his mother was involved in roaring arguments with his father, pleading with him to ease up on Andrew. Then Pa had left the house and driven away in a fury—heading, no doubt, for Coney Island.

After the evening chores, it was back to the fence, working by moonlight glowing dimly through the clouds, aided by a fading flashlight.

By midnight the moon had set and the flashlight batteries had given up. After 20 hours of exhausting work, Andrew knew that he had completed only a small fraction of the required fence. He put the tools in the basement, threw one more log into the furnace, and climbed the stone steps to the house. On the porch, he hung up his jacket, then went into the kitchen.

"I'm so sorry, Son," his mother said. "I've tried to reason with your Pa, but he . . . . he just doesn't . . . ." There were tears in her eyes as Andrew's mother held her tall son close.

"It's no good, Ma. It's no good. But thanks for trying." Andrew trudged up the stairs to his bedroom. Completely exhausted, too tired even to get undressed, he collapsed on the bed and pulled a blanket over himself.

"Dear God," he murmured. "You know I've tried. But I don't see how I can make it . . . . Can't let Julie down . . . ." And then the boy's exhausted body slid into a profound sleep, pulling his exhausted mind with it, and leaving his prayer unfinished.

Monday, December 21; after school [46 days to competition]

Mr. Lesser was doing what he did best: Proving to young musicians that pretty good is not nearly good enough.

"Again, People, from Letter 'D', at half tempo. Flutes, clarinets, oboe: Where the notes are tied, I want obligato. Where there are no tie marks, I want each note attacked individually. Horns: After the first two notes, you are on the upbeat. Now let's try it again."

The band tried it again for the four-thousandth time. "Good! Trumpets and cornets: You're carrying the melody in triad chords. But high brass will always carry; hold down the volume slightly. Saxophones: You are doubling the brass—and keeping them from sounding brassy. I want more sax, less brass . . . ."

Totally engrossed in their work, neither conductor nor band members noticed for some time that Mr. Cochran, the principal, had entered the band room and had taken a seat in the back.

"Mr. Cochran," said Mr. Lesser. "Welcome. Is there something you'd like to say to my New York Philharmonic?"

"No, not really, except that they sound great! I get phone calls from parents sometimes. Some of them wonder if you're working these kids too hard, but most of the people who call are happy to support what you—what all of you—are trying to do. I just thought I'd come in and see for myself. Now, just go ahead with your rehearsal. I'll sit here and listen, if that's all right."

The band resumed their polishing of Section "D" for their audience of one. As Mr. Cochran listened, he noticed how old and worn out the two tympani were. A small smile on his face, Mr. Cochran wrote a brief note on his clipboard.

Tuesday, December 22 [45 days to competition]

Julie's notes and her whispered words told Andrew all he needed to know. She had a beautiful new formal gown. She would be wearing her heels. She was excited beyond measure to be going on her first date ever. She would teach him to dance. He didn't need to worry about getting her a corsage. Would he like her to drive, since she could borrow her father's car?

Each time Andrew looked at Julie, he had to choke down the stifling fear that he might not finish the fence in time, that his father might not . . . . Then, fiercely he would say to himself, No! I can't think like that! Julie is counting on me. Somehow, someway, I've got to finish the fence. I can't let Julie down!"

Andrew abandoned his homework. In the upside-down priorities of his world, there was no time for homework. When hitch hiking, he found himself not walking, but running between rides. By getting up at four o'clock, he was able to get in two hours of wood cutting and fence building before morning chores and school. By rushing the milking and the other chores, he was able to find time for a few more post holes, a few more posts set. By working every night until midnight, he was able to cut down a few more trees, able to cut them up, able to make more of the required posts. Reluctantly, Andrew even shortened up on Dmitri Shostakovich at home. And he cut back to four hours' sleep a night.

Wednesday, December 23, lunch-time

At the lunch-time rehearsal Mr. Lesser announced that with school being out for the holidays, there would be no rehearsals—not even sectionals!—until after New Year's. There arose a mighty cheer from the band, whose members by now were ready for a little break.

"But," Mr. Lesser had added, "you will be expected to get in not less than two hours of practice at home every day. And I want good, hard, intense practice, not just going through the motions.

"Now, tonight is the Christmas Ball. I know some of you ladies need several hours to get ready for a formal dance, so I think that just for today we'll skip the after-school rehearsal, too."

Each band member had his or her own reason for being glad the after-school rehearsal had been canceled. Andrew Sherwood's reason was fairly simple: It meant that for the first time in weeks, he could ride the bus home—and get some more of the fence finished before the dance!

But not all of it. Though he had worked himself to complete exhaustion, Andrew saw that a large part of the pasture fence remained unfinished.

The same day; evening.

The first thing Andrew Sherwood did at home was to show his mother Julie's picture and ask his mother for her permission to return to town. Very briefly, he told her that he had promised the girl in the picture that he would take her to a dance at eight that very evening.

"Ma, I'd love to tell you all about it, but I've got so much to do before I can go. Could you maybe just iron my white shirt and try to shine my shoes and get my stuff ready for me? I promise to tell you all about it later tonight when I get home."

Delighted that her son actually was going to spend an evening with other young people, Alice Sherwood had given her permission and had cheerfully cooperated. "Son, you've worked so hard this week—I've really worried about you. Now hurry! Get your chores done quickly so you won't be late for the dance."

Andrew rushed through his chores as fast as he could. As he worked, two parts of his brain argued with each other.

"I'm going to the dance."

"No, you're not. That fence isn't finished yet."

"Pa didn't say I had to have it done by a certain time."

"He also hasn't given you permission to go to a dance."

"Maybe not. But Ma did. And what else *can* I do? Julie is counting on me. I made a promise to her, and I just can't let her down."

"The Old Man will knock you clear to Copleys' if you take off without his permission. You know that, don't you?"

"Yeah, well where's the Old Man? He isn't even here to ask or to tell me one way or the other. And I'll likely be home from the dance by the time he even gets here."

"So you're going to the dance?"

"I'm going to the dance. With Julie."

The chores finished, Andrew ran toward the house to shower and get ready for the dance. Mr. Andrew Sherwood was taking Miss Julie Ryckman to the Christmas Ball! He had never in his life been so excited or so happy.

But as he hurried up the steps to the house, Andrew saw the lights of a car turning into the Sherwood driveway. "Not Julie?" he thought. "I told her I would get to town without help, that I would meet her at her house."

The vehicle pulled to a stop. The driver turned off the lights and stepped out of the pickup.

"Evenin', Son," said Jim Sherwood.

The same day; just before midnight

Andrew Sherwood lay in the darkness in his bedroom, his large, calloused hands drawn back under his head. His eyes were open, but he made no sound, no movement.

By the dim moonlight shining through his bedroom window Andrew could make out ghostly shapes and shadows all around him. He could see the two-by-four studs in the walls and the ceiling joists overhead supporting the roofing boards. Snaking through the wooden joists was the electric cable which connected the light switch to the overhead junction box, from which hung a bare light bulb, now unlighted.

Had he bothered to sit up and turn around, Andrew could have looked out the window and seen the yard directly below, and the barn and pasture to the west. He might have made out the whiteness of dozens of newly-split fence posts around most of the pasture.

From downstairs Andrew could hear voices, the furious voices of his parents. As always, they were arguing about how to raise a son. Andrew knew—had always known—that his parents eventually would divorce, and that he would be the sole cause of the divorce. Maybe tonight would be the last straw. Maybe besides breaking Julie's heart tonight, Andrew thought, he may have destroyed his parents' marriage, too.

"But what's the harm?" his mother was pleading. "Why couldn't the boy have gone to the dance?"

"We've been all through that, Alice. I won't repeat myself."

"Jim, he's worked so hard to get all his chores done and to get that new fence up . . . . He's worked like a slave this week!"

"Doesn't matter. You can't just go out with some girl and then announce it after the fact to your Old Man."

"When would he have told you? You're always off at Coney Island drinking beer . . . ."

"Now don't start in on that, Woman! Anyway, a boy seventeen years old goin' out with some girl is just askin' for trouble . . . likely get her pregnant or something."

"You know your son better than that."

"I know he's dumb—plenty dumb enough to do something really stupid. He'll have time enough for dating and courting later, after he's out of school and has a job and can support a wife."

"Couldn't he at least have walked to Copley's and called the girl? She's sitting home thinking he didn't care enough to even give her a phone call."

"She'll find out soon enough."

"Oh, but Jim! *More* fence-building? You had to give him *another* fence to build?"

"Got to make the punishment fit the crime! Besides not asking permission to go to that fool dance, he didn't finish the fence around the pasture, so he is going to build a fence around the entire farm!"

"Jim, that is the cruelest thing I've ever heard of . . . ."

They were repeating themselves now. But it didn't matter. It was too late and then some, Andrew thought. By now Julie had learned once and for all that she couldn't count on Andrew Sherwood.

And maybe it was just as well. "Who are we kidding, to think that I could show up at her house wearing school pants and old shoes and a coat that smells like a barn, and her in some pretty dress? Who are we kidding that I could get a ride to town on a Wednesday night and then find her house and be there by eight o'clock? Who are we kidding that I could keep her from finding out that my Old Man is an alcoholic? Or that I'm dirt poor? Or that I'm as stupid and clumsy and ugly as Pa says I am?

"Naw, it's just as well that she has the hurt now instead of the embarrassment later. It's just as well that she's angry with me and ready to dump me. She'll tell me off, and that will be the end of it. And she has every right."

Andrew turned over on his bed and pulled a pillow over his head to block out the angry voices, the angry thoughts, the angry feelings. No good. Though he might block out the voices downstairs, he couldn't drive Julie's voice nor his own from his mind.

Quietly, Andrew got out of bed and opened his saxophone case. Wetting the reed between his lips, he slowly, deliberately assembled the tenor sax which might help drown out the angry voices. Then he sat on the edge of the bed, eyes closed, and began to play a moody song which must have been written for a tenor sax man with a broken heart:

> I need your love so badly;
> I love you oh so madly;
> But I don't stand a ghost of a chance with you.
> I thought at last I'd found you;
> But other loves surround you;
> And I don't stand a ghost of a chance with you . . . .
> If you'd surrender just for a tender kiss or two,
> You might discover that I'm the lover
> Meant for you—and I'd be true.
> But what's the good of scheming?
> I know I must be dreaming,
> 'Cause I don't stand a ghost of a chance with you.

Big boys don't cry. But sometimes their tenor saxes do.

7
The Gift

***Thursday, December 24; late afternoon** [43 days to competition]*

As Alice Sherwood strained the milk through a clean dishtowel, Andrew arranged fruit tree trimmings in a fruit jar filled with water.

"It isn't much, Ma . . . but, well, this is for you. Merry Christmas."

Alice Sherwood considered the odd gift. "Why, thank you, Son. That's very pretty."

"Mr. Goodmanson says fruit tree twigs will bloom right in the middle of winter if you'll put them in water and leave them in a warm, sunny place by a window. He says they should blossom out in a week or so."

"Blossoms in winter . . . what a nice thought. Thank you, Son. It's a lovely Christmas present."

Andrew looked at the kitchen clock. "Ma? It's Christmas Eve . . . . Maybe I'd better start for town . . . to get Pa."

"It's still early, Son. Even if you found Pa now, he probably wouldn't let you drive him home until later."

"Well, I was hoping to get to a store before they close. Maybe get a Christmas present for . . . ." Andrew did not to say her name. The memory of last evening's disappointment was still an open wound.

"Do you have any money?"

"Not much, Ma. But maybe enough."

"For your friend? The girl you were going to meet at the dance last night?"

Andrew nodded, but said nothing.

"That's good, Son. Maybe you'll see her, tell her what happened last night—why you couldn't take her to the dance . . . . She'll want to know. I'm sure she'll understand."

"I don't think I could tell her, Ma . . . ."

"No, perhaps not . . . . Here, I've got a little bit of milk and egg money stashed away. It's only a couple of dollars, but maybe it will help."

"I . . . I can't take that, Ma. You need that for groceries."

"It's all right, Son. You work such long hours and you never get any allowance. You take these two dollars and get something nice for your . . . friend."

"Thanks. Thanks, Ma."

"Now, you'd better hurry. The stores will close early on Christmas Eve. I hope you can get a ride to town. And after you deliver your present, find your Pa and get him home safe." Alice Sherwood gave a warm embrace to the son who towered over her.

As Andrew started down the driveway, he took the pocket-knife from his jacket pocket, and cut a few long twigs from each of several fruit trees. Then, twigs in hand, he strode toward Ferguson Road.

Some time later Andrew got out of a car in town and thanked the driver for the ride. The driver called, "Merry Christmas," and turned onto the old arching bridge which connects Oregon City with West Linn across the river. Andrew hurried to a drug store which was just closing.

"I'm sorry, young man. We're closed." It was clear that the sales clerk was not interested in making one more sale.

"But, I've *got* to buy one thing. Please?."

"It's six o'clock. We close at six."

"But—"

The owner of the store appeared. "Is there a problem here?"

Andrew spoke first. "Sir? I . . . I won't be but a minute. I need to buy a vase."

The store owner spoke to the clerk. "It's all right. Let him in." The clerk, irritated by this violation of company policy, complied, then locked the door behind Andrew.

"Thank you, Sir," said Andrew to the store owner. "I had a hard time getting a ride to town, and I . . . ."

"It's all right. You said you were looking for a vase?"

"Yes, Sir. Something nice to hold these flowers."

The store owner looked at the odd collection of twigs.

"Oh, they're not flowers yet, just twigs from our fruit trees. But in a few weeks . . . ."

The store owner laughed. "I see. Well, then, a vase for next month's apple blossoms."

"Not just apple blossoms, Sir. Apricots, peaches, plums, all kinds of blossoms."

"How about this one?" The man held up a tall, white vase. "This should look nice with your blossoms."

"Yes, Sir, I believe it would. Sir? I've . . . I've only got $2.48 . . . ."

The store owner looked at the price tag, then at Andrew. He hesitated for a moment, then removed the price tag and put it in his pocket. "Now there's a coincidence," he said. "This vase goes for exactly $2.48. Merry Christmas, young man. I hope the person who gets this really enjoys it."

"Yes, Sir. Thank you, Sir. And Merry Christmas to you, Sir." The store owner unlocked the door and Andrew left.

Christmas Eve; evening

Andrew had never been to Julie's home before, but she had told him how to get there—a hundred years ago when she still had liked him and had waited in vain for him to take her to the Christmas Ball.

What reception would he get now? Would she simply slap his face and slam the door? Or would she tell him off first, and then throw him and his stupid twigs off the porch?

Or would it be her father who threw him out and told him off?

Whatever. Andrew had disappointed Julie, and he was ready to take whatever medicine she prescribed for him. She deserved at least this—the chance to get even and to get him out of her life.

Fearfully, Andrew knocked on the door. From inside he could hear the sound of a phonograph playing Christmas music.

It was Alton Ryckman who opened the door. "Good evening."

"Good evening, Sir. I . . . Is . . . I mean . . . Is Julie here, Sir?"

"Why, no, you just missed her. She's out delivering some presents to her sister's family.

Andrew looked both relieved and disappointed. "I see . . . ."

Mr. Ryckman knew instinctively that this tall young man at his door was the cause of last evening's many tears. By the same instinct, he knew that this shy lad had not purposely stood his daughter up.

"But, listen, Julie should be back soon. Won't you come in and wait for her by the fire, maybe try out some of her Christmas cookies?"

"I . . . I'd like that, Sir . . . but . . . but I can't . . . I can't stay." It was difficult for Andrew to get the words out.

"You know, I could call her on the phone and tell her you're here."

"I . . . That would be nice, Sir . . . but I . . . well, I . . . I guess I'd better just leave my present and go. I need to . . . you know, I . . . I need to apologize to her . . . but . . . I have something still that I've got to . . . got to take care of . . . ."

"Well, I'll be happy to tell Julie you were here, and to give her your present."

"Sir? Maybe you could . . . could put some water in this vase for me . . . and give it to Julie tomorrow morning for Christmas? I . . . I wasn't able to get it wrapped in pretty paper or anything, and it isn't much, but . . . . Tell her to put the vase by a window in a sunny place indoors, and . . . and in a week or so she'll have a nice bouquet of flowers."

"Yes, I'll tell her. And your name is . . . ."

"Just . . . just tell her it's from a friend . . . a friend in the band, Sir . . . ."

"All right. You're sure you wouldn't like to come in and wait? I know Julie would want to talk with you and receive the gift from *you*."

"No . . . . No, Sir. I've . . . I've got something important to take care of still."

Alton Ryckman felt a surge of compassion for the tall youth on the porch. He shook Andrew's hand warmly, and said, "Merry Christmas to you, Son. I'm sure Julie will be very pleased with your present." As Andrew turned to leave, Mr. Ryckman quietly closed the door, a gentle smile on his face.

From Julie's home, Andrew walked down the hill toward the railroad tracks. "The Old Man goes to Coney Island to drink with others," he reasoned aloud. "But on Christmas Eve he always drinks alone. Better check out these other joints along the way."

Andrew approached a bar with "Blitz-Weinhardt" and "Olympia" neon signs in the windows. From inside came the sound of loud laughter above the music from a jukebox.

Andrew entered and approached the bartender.

"Who? Jim Sherwood? I don't think so. Hank? You recall if Jim Sherwood was here earlier tonight?" The bartender shrugged his shoulders. "Can't say for sure, Boy. Might have been. You tried across the street?"

"I looked in their window. Didn't see him . . . . Well, thanks. I'll stop by later if I don't find him . . . ."

"That's fine. And Merry Christmas."

"Yeah. Merry Christmas." Andrew left, walking through a cold drizzle to another bar down the street.

"Hey, Kid . . . . No one under 21 is allowed in here. Now, scram!"

"I'm . . . I'm not here to buy drinks, Sir. I'm looking for my Pa."

"It's all the same to the State Agency people. They see you in here, I lose my license."

"My Pa, Sir . . . his name is Jim. Jim Sherwood. Has he been here tonight?"

"Who? Jim? Naw. Ain't seen him tonight. Now you better scram, Kid. I got enough trouble."

"Yeah. Well, thanks. I don't want to cause you trouble."

As Andrew left, he bumped into a loud couple full of Christmas cheer. He walked along a well-lit but mostly deserted street, too preoccupied to notice the colorful Christmas decorations, the store window displays and the garlands on the light poles.

At the end of the street Andrew came to the Coney Island Bar. Andrew first checked the small parking lot at the side of the tavern.

"Now we're getting close, Folks. There's the Old Man's pickup."

Andrew entered the bar and stood for a moment, scanning the crowd, looking for his father. Then he walked to a corner table, where Jim Sherwood sat alone, with several empty beer bottles before him on the table.

Andrew sat down at the table opposite his father. "Evening, Pa."

"Evenin', Son. Figured you'd be gettin' here pretty soon." Andrew gauged by the extent of his father's slurred speech that he was well into his annual Christmas drunk.

"Yeah, Pa."

Jim Sherwood spoke quietly, without feeling. "Christmas again. Merry Christmas. Ho, ho, ho."

There was a long pause before Andrew asked, "How come, Pa? How come is Christmas always . . . you know?"

"How come? I don't know. I guess it's remembering Christmas with a step-dad who . . . ."

Andrew waited a long time before prompting his father. "A step-dad who . . . ?"

Jim Sherwood pried the cap off one more bottle of Oly. "You really want to know?" he asked.

"Yeah, Pa. I really would like to know."

For a long time Jim considered whether to explain or not. "Christmas means watching your step-dad come home drunk and then . . . ."

Andrew waited. He had been this far with his father so many times before.

"Christmas means watching your blasted stepfather . . . ."

Again Andrew waited. So much time passed that he began to wonder if his father had simply lost his train of thought. "Christmas, Pa. Tell me why Christmas is always . . . the worst day of the year."

"Naw. Ain't no use in it. Ain't no use in speakin' evil of the dead. Let's forget it."

Jim leaned forward as if to confide a great secret to his son. "But I will tell you this: I have found a way to forget how that rotten old man treated me and my ma and my little sister. It really works." Jim held up his bottle of beer.

Andrew said nothing. There was quite simply nothing he could say. There was silence until Jim had finished his Oly.

Then Andrew changed subjects. "Pa? About last night . . . ."

"Son, I feel so bad about that. I don't know *why* I act like that sometimes. All day today I been thinkin' of how I should have been glad to see my boy goin' off to a dance with his friends. And instead I acted like some kind of horse's behind . . . ."

"It's all right, Pa. Maybe it's better this way. No use in some girl thinking she might like me."

"Why? She too good for my boy? If she thinks she's too good for my boy, then who needs her?" The words came out quietly, no anger in them.

Jim Sherwood drained one more Oly before Andrew spoke again. "Pa? Why don't we stop on the hill above the house and cut a Christmas tree? We could take it home to Ma. We . . . you and me and Ma . . . we could trim it and maybe make some popcorn. I think it would make Ma happy."

Through a drunken haze Jim Sherwood considered what his son had suggested. "Yeah. You're right, Son. We'll do 'er." But Andrew knew there would be no Christmas tree, no popcorn, no happy time together as a family.

"Here . . . .you help me get out to the pickup. I'm feelin' a little woozy. Maybe you'd better drive, Son."

The cold drizzle had turned to a heavy rain as Andrew helped his father to the pickup. All the way home Jim Sherwood slept, his head resting on Andrew's shoulder.

Andrew parked the pickup in the driveway, and then carried his father up the stone steps to the house. Christmas had come once again to the Sherwood home.

Friday, December 25; afternoon [42 days to competition]

On Wednesday, Andrew had failed to show up for the Christmas Ball, and Julie had decided she hated him. On Thursday, he had brought her a Christmas present, and she had decided she loved him after all. Now it was Friday—Christmas—and she didn't know what to think.

If he didn't like her, why had he asked her to go to the dance in the first place? And if he did like her, why had he stood her up without even a phone call? But if he didn't like her, why had he brought her a Christmas present? But if he liked her, why had he not waited for her when he delivered the present? The questions went around and around in Julie's head—but none of the answers made any sense.

On Christmas night Julie began to get some answers. She had gone to Carole's home to spend the evening with her best friend—and to talk about what Santa had brought good flute players and oboe players. While they listened to Carole's new stereo record albums and tried on their new sweaters, the two girls talked.

"Did you know I called you Wednesday evening?" Carole asked Julie.

"I . . . I was busy and couldn't come to the phone."

"I know. Your father told me. Something about you getting ready for the Christmas Ball."

"He told you that?"

Carole nodded. "And did you know I called again later that same night?"

Julie said nothing.

"This time your father said you weren't feeling very well. He said you had gone to bed early."

There was a very long pause. Then very gently Carole said, "Julie, I'm your best friend. When you want to talk about it, I'll be here to listen and to try to help."

Julie's eyes filled with tears, and she began to cry softly. Carole cradled her weeping friend in her arms and said the reassuring words Julie's dead mother might have said. Finally, Julie spoke, and the whole story came tumbling out: "I'm . . . I'm sorry I've been such a goose. But if I haven't told you everything, it's not because I didn't trust you. But there is a boy —you know him. He's in the band—and he's shy—and I was afraid if others knew I liked him, it would make it harder for him, and I . . . ."

"It's Andrew Sherwood, isn't it." Carole knew the answer to her own question.

Julie was genuinely surprised. "How did you know? I haven't told anyone . . . ."

"Goose. Where do I spend more time than in band? And who would I watch more in band than my best friend? And wouldn't I be blind to not see how you look at Andrew Sherwood? Wouldn't I be even more blind to not see how he blushes when you look at him?"

"I . . . I didn't think anyone had noticed."

"I don't suppose anyone else has. Only me."

"But Carole, I'm so confused. First he asks me to the dance, then he doesn't show up. What am I supposed to think? Then the next evening he comes to my door—while I'm away!—and leaves a Christmas present. What am I supposed to think? I write notes to him, but he almost never writes back. He never comes to any of the dances. He never calls me. I gave him my picture, but he hasn't given me his in return. Oh, Carole, it's such a mess! It doesn't make any sense."

"It would make perfectly good sense if you knew the whole story."

"The whole story? Right. And where shall I go to get the whole story?"

"To your best friend."

Julie looked puzzled. "*You* know something about Andrew that I don't?"

Carole was slightly smug. "Of course. I could have told you a long time ago, if you had asked."

"Like what? And how do you know about Andrew?"

"My father happens to be a carpenter. He happens to work every day with Andrew's father. And my mother buys milk and eggs from Andrew's mother twice a week. Come to think of it, I've been with my mother a couple of times when we were in Andrew's kitchen.

"And I just happen to have a note which Andrew once wrote to you and then threw away." Carole handed Julie the crumpled paper.

Quickly, Julie read the note. Then she read it again, slowly. "Yes," she said quietly. "This really does help explain a lot of things. I'm beginning to see why Andrew is so shy, why he acts the way he does."

Before the evening ended, Julie sat in the living room with Carole and her parents and listened as Carole skillfully guided the conversation to the Sherwoods. Without ever knowing why, Mr. and Mrs. Larsen told Carole and Julie many things which, together with the crumpled note, helped Julie make perfectly good sense of Andrew Sherwood's behavior.

Before she fell asleep, Julie recounted in her mind all that she had learned this evening about Andrew Sherwood. Andrew's great physical size and strength resulted from endless hours of hard labor at home. Andrew spent his Saturdays actually digging stumps out of the ground. Andrew's shyness resulted from years of being screamed at and ridiculed and abused. Andrew's maturity resulted from having to be the "man of the house" in a home where alcohol had taken away the real man of the house. Andrew had neither telephone nor transportation nor spending money. Andrew spent each Christmas Eve going from one bar to another in search of his father. Andrew could never afford to buy copies of his class pictures. Andrew was the single most polite, most hard-working, most decent boy in the county. Andrew would never do anything dishonest or dishonorable . . . .

As Julie was drifting into sleep, the words from one of her new records ran through her mind.

> It had to be you. It had to be you.
> I wandered around, finally found somebody who
> Could make me be true—could make me be blue,
> And even be glad just to be sad, thinking of you.
> Some others I've found might still hang around;
> Might never be cross or try to be boss, but they
>   wouldn't do:
> For nobody else gave me a thrill. Without your charms,
>   I'd love you still:
> It had to be you, wonderful you: It had to be you.

As welcome sleep gently overtook her, Julie whispered "Andrew, will you forgive me for doubting you? Andrew, I think maybe I'm really in love with you."

Tuesday, January 5; Second Period [32 days to competition]

In every high school physics class there comes a day of reckoning. For Carole Larsen and Martin Strong the day of reckoning was Tuesday, January 5. Mr. Goodmanson's neat printing on the chalkboard detailed the reckoning: "Physics Term Projects, due January 5."

Martin walked to the front of the classroom, where he opened his French horn case. As he fitted the mouthpiece to his instrument, Carole Larsen was assembling her flute. They took time to make sure the instruments were in tune, then Martin said, "For our physics project, Carole and I would like to provide a practical demonstration of sound-wave dynamics."

Then, playing from memory, the two young people played the incredible duet from Letter "G" of the Fifth Symphony. As Carole played the delicate eighth-note counterpoint essential to maintaining the rhythm, Martin played a mournful slow-motion song of sadness from the haunted forests of Russia.

The music was beautiful, the execution perfect. But Mr. Goodmanson was incredulous. "That's it? That's your physics project for this term?"

"We—the band is working really hard to get ready for the State Competition, Mr. Goodmanson. We haven't had much time for anything else for quite a while." It was Carole, turning on the charm, hoping against hope that Mr. Goodmanson—"Badmonson" some called him—might have mercy on her and on Martin.

"Really, Sir," added Martin. "We've been practicing pretty much night and day . . . . And I might add that musical tones which sound good together have compatible sound-wave frequencies which . . . ."

Mr. Goodmanson cut him off impatiently. "I know. I know all that. Don't try to snow me, Martin. The fact is that neither you nor Carole have prepared a real term project."

"I really enjoyed the demonstration of sound-wave dynamics," said another student—a member of the band. "It sounds like Carole and Martin have worked really hard on their project."

Grudgingly, Mr. Goodmanson agreed. "It did sound very nice." He looked for a long time at Carole and Martin before continuing: "I'll make you a deal. If the band takes State, you both get an "A" for this alleged physics project. If the band doesn't take State, you both get a 'D minus'."

Late December

For most of the students in the band, the time between Christmas and New Years' was devoted to relaxing and having fun with their friends——plus two hours of intensive practice on their musical instruments each day. There were movies to see, parties to attend, ski runs to explore, records to play, telephone calls to make. There were even television programs to watch on the small black and white screens which were beginning to appear in some living rooms.

For Andrew Sherwood, the holidays were devoted to solving an interesting math problem: A certain high-school senior has to build a fence around three acres of pasture, plus another fence around an irregularly-shaped eleven acre farm. For 250 feet the same fence will do for both projects. If the fence posts must be six feet apart, how many posts will the boy need? And if each post is eight feet long, how many hundred-foot trees will he need to cut down and work up to obtain the necessary posts? And if all of the thirty-inch post holes were laid end to end, how many times would they reach to China and back?

And if the boy had a heavy load of other work which had to continue, and if all Saturdays were devoted to rooting stumps out of the pasture, and if the boy had two hours a day of practice on his saxophone, how could he ever hope to get it all done?

Some math problem! thought Andrew. I wish someone else would solve this one.

But there was no one else—only Andrew Sherwood. And if not now, when? After school resumed in January, it would only get worse. Each day of his Christmas "vacation" Andrew arose before the sun and worked until there was no longer any daylight, felling trees and turning them into fence posts, digging post holes, setting posts, transferring barbed wire to the new posts. And for a break, he milked cows and chopped fire wood and did his other chores.

8
The Bassoon

Friday, January 8; evening [28 days to competition]

It had been a perfectly wonderful day at Mount Hood. Jack Stephenson and Arlene Simmons had decided to ditch all their classes and just spend the day skiing on the sun-swept slopes above Timberline Lodge. The snow had been perfect, the new skis perfect, the beautiful new ski clothes and ski boots perfect. Arlene had enjoyed every minute of it.

And in the evening Jack had taken her to the restaurant in the lodge for a prime rib dinner with all the trimmings.

Sitting by a warm fireplace big enough to drive a truck into, Arlene marvelled at the beauty and grandeur of the old Lodge's stonework, its huge wooden pillars, and its high ceilings under log rafters.

"I don't suppose," she said to Jack, "that there is any place in all the world I'd rather be right now than right here."

Jack poured a glass of wine for Arlene and one for himself. "Not even in the band room at Oregon City High?"

"Oh, that!" she scoffed. "I should be in that stupid band room for a Friday night sectional rehearsal? When I could be at Timberline Lodge skiing and eating prime rib? Not likely!"

"Ah, but the training rules . . . ." Jack reminded her. "Didn't Old Man Lesser say anyone missing a rehearsal would be cut from band?"

"Of course he did. But the Fifth Symphony has a bugger of a bassoon part, and I'm the only bassoon player he has—and I know my part perfectly. What's he going to do if I miss a rehearsal or two? Throw me out of band? If he kicks me out, he shoots the whole competition."

"So you've got it all figured out, Arlene. You can forget the rules and just do what you like."

"I *always* do just what I like. I've never found a rule I couldn't bluff my way past."

Jack lifted his wine glass in a toast to Arlene.

Monday, January 11,; first period [*25 days to competition*]

As the bell rang and the members of the band left for their other classes, Mr. Lesser called Arlene into his office.

"Miss Simmons, you are aware that you missed all of your rehearsals on Friday?"

"I was sick."

"And that you missed the Friday night woodwind sectional?"

"Yes, Sir, because I had the flu. I couldn't make it Friday."

"Miss Simmons, Oregon City is a small town. Everybody pretty well knows everybody else's business. You weren't sick."

Arlene changed tactics. "Well, what of it? I know my part. I can play the bassoon part with my eyes closed. Why should I have to sit in the band room on a Friday night while the idiot oboes and saxophones learn what they should have learned at home?"

"I'm not here to debate the fine art of instrumental music pedagogy with you, Miss Simmons. You're finished. You're out. I'll arrange to have you transferred to first period study hall."

Arlene was stunned. "You can't do this!"

"I can't do what?"

"You can't kick me out of band! I'm the only bassoon player you've got. You'll shoot the whole competition if there's no bassoon part. It wouldn't be fair to the others."

"It wouldn't be fair!" Mr. Lesser was furious. "Would it be fair to hold the others to a strict set of training rules while you go your merry way skiing at Mount Hood? *They* should rehearse for two hours on a Friday night while you and Jack Stephenson are relaxing by the fire at Timberline Lodge?"

Again Arlene changed tactics. Very humbly she said, "You're right. I was a fool. Give me another chance. I won't miss rehearsal again. I promise."

"I don't give second chances, Miss Simmons. You knew the rules. Now, you'd better move it, or you'll be late for Second Period. Would you please close the door as you leave?"

Arlene stood, her teeth clenched in a controlled fury for several seconds, then wheeled and stalked out of Mr. Lesser's office, slamming the door as she left.

Wearily, Ervin Lesser closed his eyes and shook his head.

Same day, lunch-time

As the members of the band finished eating their lunches and prepared to rehearse, Mr. Lesser turned off the phonograph recording of the Fifth Symphony and called the group to order.

Very quietly he announced, "You may have noticed that we lost one of our people today. Miss Simmons won't be with us any more." The students in the band room looked at each other, most of them fully aware of the circumstances. Remarkably, most were relieved to know that Ervin Lesser would enforce his training rules.

"Now we've got a problem. We *must* have that bassoon part, and that means we need someone to replace Miss Simmons.

"What I need right now is someone who really knows how to work, someone who can get a ten-week job done in twenty-five days. Someone I can really count on."

Mr. Lesser turned and faced Andrew. "Mr. Sherwood, people tell me that you know how to work. Is that so?"

The great terror of Andrew Sherwood's life was that he might be called upon to speak in front of a group. Try as he might, no words would come out in answer to the band leader's question.

Mr. Lesser announced his decision: "Twenty-five days from now Mr. Sherwood will play the bassoon part in the state band competition."

Many members of the band had never heard Andrew Sherwood's voice. They heard it now—a halting voice expressing complete astonishment: "Sir? I . . . Did you . . . Did you mean *me*? I . . . I can't play the bassoon."

"You won't be playing a bassoon, Mr. Sherwood. You'll play the bassoon part on a baritone sax."

"But I've never . . . I've never played a baritone sax either."

"No problem. The fingering is identical to your tenor. Now, there is a baritone sax in the storage room, Mr. Sherwood. Would you get it, please?"

Andrew, aware that all eyes in the room were on him, walked to the storage room, opened the baritone sax case, put the reed in his mouth, and assembled the instrument. He adjusted the neck strap, and returned to his seat.

"Wrong seat, Mr. Sherwood. From now on you'll sit with the double reeds." Mr. Lesser indicated Arlene's now empty chair—the chair next to Julie Ryckman.

"Now, Mr. Sherwood, if you'll just play the bassoon score in two sharps and pretend that it's in the treble clef, you'll do just fine. All right, People, let's turn to Letter "N" in your score, and go to work."

As Mr. Lesser talked, Andrew rose from his seat, then glanced for an instant at Julie, who caught his eye and watched him with a small suppressed smile. As Andrew made his way to his new seat, he was careful not to look at the oboe player, who from now on would be sitting only inches from him.

Same day; in Mr. Goodmanson's class

Andrew was supposed to be doing algebra story problems. Very quietly he opened a small folded note, making sure that no one would see.

> Dear Andrew—
>
> See? Even Shostakovich thinks we should sit together. Sooner or later I'm going to get you on a dance floor. Sooner or later we're going to go on dates together. You'll see.
>
> Andrew Sherwood, the more I watch you and the more I learn about you, the more I like you. I think I like you a lot.
>
> Love, Julie

A slow, shy grin began at the right corner of Andrew Sherwood's mouth and spread until it covered his whole face.

Wednesday, January 13; Seventh Period [23 days to competition]

Coach Shelton blew his whistle and called the members of Oregon City's varsity basketball team to the bench. "All right, guys, let's take five."

The boys sat, some on the floor, some on the bench, around the coach. "You're starting to look like a basketball team, boys. I can't believe how far you've come in these past few weeks."

"You think we can take West Linn, Coach?"

"If you can keep up this same intensity? Yes."

From the bench came a quiet voice—the voice of a young man speaking adult thoughts, and hoping no one would make the connection: "We can beat West Linn if we want to badly enough."

"Swenson? What does that mean?"

"That's what Mr. Lesser told us in band, Coach. He said if we want something enough to pay the price . . . well, that nobody could keep us from having it. Only, we have to want it more and practice more than the guys in the other schools. That's what he said."

Coach Shelton thought about that. "He's right, you know." Then, half to himself, the coach said, "I wonder if this guy Shostakovich is tall enough to play center for us."

Thursday, January 14; evening *[22 days to competition]*

It was late evening when Jim Sherwood stopped the pickup in the driveway and turned off the motor. As he stepped out of the vehicle, he could hear the sound of a baritone saxophone coming from the upstairs bedroom.

"Damnable racket," he muttered. "Why can't the kid do something useful around here, instead of making that awful noise?"

As he ate his dinner, Jim Sherwood looked through the day's mail. "What's this from the high school?" he asked.

"It's a progress report on Andrew," his wife started, "but . . . ."

"Late with homework?" Jim Sherwood exploded. "Asleep in class?"

"Jim, you've been working the boy pretty hard, and he . . . ."

"That's a crock! He has time to sit on his butt and suck on that saxophone! But he's late with his homework? He's sleeping in class?"

"Jim, listen to me. The boy has to learn a new part on a new instrument. It's taking a lot of his time."

"And that stupid racket is more important than homework? I will put a stop to *that* right now!"

"You will not! That boy has no time at all for himself. He works like a slave for you. He works like a slave for Mr. Lesser. What more do you expect from him?"

"I expect that he will put first things first and get good grades! That's what I expect!"

"Yes, Jim. Yes, grades are important. Yes, it's important that the boy learn to work. But it's important that he be part of a group, too—something like band. It's important that he spend some time with other young people."

"That's another crock! If he can't get good grades, he will *not* be in the band. I'm done fooling around with that lazy, stupid kid! I am going to put an end to this band nonsense right now!"

The door to the stairs opened and Andrew appeared, baritone saxophone in hand.

"You won't need to, Pa. I'll get the homework done. I'll keep the grades up. I promise."

"You promise! What good is the promise of a stupid, lazy blockhead? I want *results!* I will accept nothing less than straight A's"!

"And if I get straight A's, Pa?"

Jim Sherwood relented slightly. "All right. All right. If you can carry straight A's, you can stay with the band. But I want a written report every Friday from every teacher that says you are getting your homework done—and that you're not falling asleep in class—and that you are doing 'A' work."

"You'll have it, Pa."

"And no slacking off on the chores."

Andrew nodded.

"And you'll give me a hundred percent on Saturdays rooting out stumps."

Andrew drew a deep breath, then nodded again.

"And the new fence?"

"I'll get the new fence in, too, Pa."

"And one other thing: If you really have to make that awful saxophone racket, do it when I'm not home!"

Friday, January 15; First Period *[21 days to competition]*

"People," Mr. Lesser began, "three weeks from today we are going to get on the bus and drive to Portland. There we will enter the Oregon State 4-A Band Competition. It is our express goal and desire to be judged Best in State." My personal goal is to score 100—with not a single demerit.

"We've been working night and day for six weeks—with time out for Christmas—on one piece of music. We have gone from awful to bad to fair to good to very good.

"But 'very good' won't do. We've still got to reach 'excellent' and then 'outstanding' and then 'superior.' Because, People, it's going to take a 'superior' to do it.

"Now, what does that mean for you? It means you've got to give it your absolute best, whether you are here in the band room or practicing at home. Some of you need a lot more work. Some of you are a long way from 'superior.' You may need to give up some movies, some dates, some telephone time, some 'sleeping-in' time.

"If you really want to take State—and you all said you did—then you've got to make this your top priority. This has to come ahead of everything else in your life. I know I've asked a lot from you; and now I'm going to ask even more. The party's over, People. Now we're going to get down to work."

And that's the way it was in the band room. Each day, each rehearsal was given to a hard, driving, demanding work-out with a slave-driver of a band leader. Every day was one more day in the crucible, burning out the dross, leaving only the pure gold.

"Now, Mr. Sherwood, what I've said to everyone else about extra work applies especially to you, because everything you have learned in the first six weeks is down the drain—gone. It doesn't matter that you had the tenor sax part down cold. All of us are depending on *you* to have the bassoon part down cold, too. Mr. Sherwood, you will have to show us that you really do know how to work."

There was a long pause before the band leader spoke again: "Mr. Sherwood, I'm going to have to ask for *all* of your time."

Same day; late evening

The woodwind sectional was nearly over. As Mr. Lesser worked with the band members on their music, a number of parents began to arrive, coats and rain hats in hand. It was apparent that it must be raining heavily outdoors.

"Again, People, from Letter 'N,' and at full tempo. Listen to each other. Watch the timing. Give me good solid notes, each precisely begun and precisely ended, thus . . . ." Mr. Lesser demonstrated vocally what he wanted from them. "Ready . . .begin!"

The woodwinds began at *fortissimo*, the tempo driving, relentless. Occasionally Mr. Lesser would speak:

"Good! Except you're letting the tempo creep up."

"With *feeling*, People. It won't sound angry unless you *feel* angry!"

"Good! Excellent! Watch the tempo!"

And then it was nine o'clock. "That will do it for tonight. Good work-out, People! It's sounding so much better. Don't forget your practicing at home. And I'll see you Monday morning early!"

Quickly, the members of the section put away their instruments, and left with the parents who had come to pick them up. Julie gave her father a hug, then turned to Andrew.

"Andrew, you've met my father, I think."

"Yes . . . I'm . . . I'm very happy to . . . . It's nice to see you again, Sir."

"And I'm glad to see you again, too, Andrew. I understand you're learning the bassoon part now."

"Yes, Sir . . . . I hope so, Sir." There was an awkward pause, then, "If . . . if you'll excuse me, Sir . . . I . . . I've got to hurry home now."

Mr. Ryckman laughed. "What's the hurry? It's Friday night. I thought maybe you'd like to join Julie and me for a hamburger and a milk shake."

Julie put one hand on Andrew's arm. "Please?"

There it was again: the terror in his eyes—only maybe not as bad as in the past. "I . . . . Thank you . . . both of you. But . . . well, I . . . I just *have* to hurry home."

Mr. Ryckman chuckled. "At nine o'clock? What's so pressing at nine o'clock on a Friday night, Andrew?"

"I . . . My Dad . . . well, Sir . . . I . . . I still have cows to milk."

"Cows to milk! I milked a few myself when I was your age and living in Michigan! Well, we can't keep you from your chores. Maybe another time?"

"But your folks aren't . . . you don't have a ride yet." Julie knew there would be no one to pick Andrew up, but she didn't want to hurt Andrew by letting him know it. "Your parents . . . ."

Andrew replied too quickly. "Oh, they'll be here soon . . . . I . . . I'm sure they'll be here soon. I'll just start down the road . . . and they'll . . . ." The sentence trailed off. Andrew was unable to complete the lie.

Mr. Ryckman looked at Andrew, compassion on his face. "Would you let us drive you home, Son? For the cows' sake, I mean?"

Andrew smiled gratefully. Julie, delighted, squeezed Andrew's arm, causing his face to turn red.

As Mr. Ryckman drove through the black night, his windshield wipers could barely keep pace with the pouring rain. Julie sat between her father and this tall boy whom she had been pursuing for six weeks.

In the darkness Julie snuggled close to Andrew, and squeezed his arm with one hand. Andrew found this to be at once both very pleasant and very alarming. He was glad that it was dark so that no one could see either the delight or the terror on his face.

"Say, you live quite a ways out of town, young man."

Andrew swallowed hard. "Yes, Sir. Seven miles, Sir."

"Seven miles is a pretty good hike for a boy on a black, rainy night. I'm surprised your folks would let you walk . . . ."

"My Pa . . . . My Pa has the pickup, and he . . . . He isn't home from work yet."

"What sort of work does your father do that keeps him out this late on a Friday night?"

"He's a carpenter."

"A carpenter . . . . I see." Mr. Ryckman did not see. All the carpenters he knew worked fairly regular day-time hours and were at home on Friday evenings.

Julie tried to defuse the uncomfortable silence. "Daddy's editor of *The Enterprise*."

"That's right. I got out of the cow-milking business as soon as I could!"

"Yes, Sir. I can understand that! I turn right at this next road here, Sir. Our house is a mile down Ferguson Road."

Mr. Ryckman turned the car onto the gravel road. "I hope your chores won't keep you out in this frog-flusher for too long . . . ."

"About an hour or so, Sir. I've got the two cows to milk, some chickens to feed, the eggs to gather, some firewood to chop for the furnace. It won't take long."

Andrew had just gotten to where he felt somewhat comfortable having Julie's hand on his arm. And then she slipped her soft hand into his huge, calloused hand, and gave it a little squeeze. In the darkness no one could see that Andrew's pulse had risen to 148 or that all the blood in his entire body was located north of his chin. The one thing that saved him was that he didn't have to say anything for a few minutes.

"This . . . this is our place—here on the right," he managed. Mr. Ryckman turned his car into the gravel driveway.

Seeing car lights, Andrew's mother appeared at the window of the farmhouse. Julie gave Andrew's hand one more squeeze before he got out of the car.

"Will you call me later?" she asked, again knowing what the answer would be—but hoping anyway.

"I would, Julie . . . . Really, I'd call you . . . if we had a phone. And Mr. Ryckman? Thank you, Sir. Thank you for the ride home . . . ."

Reluctantly, Andrew disengaged his hand from Julie's and ran through the rain toward the house and his chores.

Neither Andrew nor the two cows needed light to get the milking done. In the darkness of the small barn the two cows munched their hay and grain. In the darkness Andrew filled both milk pails with warm, foaming milk. Tonight as he worked, Andrew serenaded the two animals in a rich, warm baritone voice:

> The snow is snowing, the wind is blowing,
> But I can weather the storm.
> What do I care how much it may storm?
> I've got my love to keep me warm!
> I can't remember a worse December,
> Just watch those icicles form,
> What do I care if icicles form?
> I've got my love to keep me warm!

> Off with my overcoat; off with my gloves;
> I need no overcoat: I'm burnin' with love.
> My heart's on fire; the flame grows higher,
> So I will weather the storm.
> What do I care how much it may storm?
> I've got my love to keep me warm!

Sunday, January 17; midnight *[19 days to competition]*

Andrew was in his bedroom, plowing through the bassoon part on his baritone sax when his mother opened the door.

"How's it coming, Son?"

"I don't know, Ma. I hope I can handle it . . . but it will take a lot of time and a lot of work."

"I'm sure you can do it, Son."

"If I had six weeks more, I *know* I could play this part right, but all I've got is three."

"It sounds good to me. I'm sure you can do it. And I'm proud that Mr. Lesser has entrusted you with such an important assignment."

"Yeah, Ma. But I'm scared. What if I can't cut it? What if we come up short at the competition because of *me*? What will the other kids say?"

"Don't think about failure, Andrew. Think of success and then work for it."

"Either way, it takes *time*, and I haven't got much of that. I mean, from four in the morning on it's building fence and doing chores. Then it's school and then it's band and then it's walking home and then it's more fence and more chores. On Saturdays it's rooting out stumps.

"By the time I get to my homework and my practicing, I'm so tired I can't stay awake. If I don't practice hard, I let Mr. Lesser and the whole band down. If I *do* practice, then it's the Old Man who's climbing up the front of me and walking down the back.

"And, everybody's supposed to practice not less than two hours a day—except me. I'm supposed to practice all day and all night."

"You'll do fine, Son. Now, you'd better get some sleep. Morning comes early around here."

"That's the truth! All right, Ma. I'll just practice a little longer, then knock it off."

"Good night, Son." Alice arose and started for the door. "I'm very proud of you, Son. And I love you very much."

"I know that, Ma. And I love you, too. But, Ma? You reckon Pa . . . . you reckon he hates me?"

A look of deep concern clouded Alice's face. She closed the door and returned to her son. "No, Son," she said quietly. "Your Pa doesn't hate you. He loves you as much as I do."

"How do you figure that, Ma? He won't let me play football or other sports. He hassles me about the band. He wouldn't let me take Julie to the Christmas Ball. He yells at me and swears at me and calls me names . . . ."

"Yes. But how does he treat you when he's drunk?"

Andrew thought about that. The gentle, soft-spoken man in the drunken haze loved his son, and Andrew couldn't deny it.

"Your father loves you very much, Andrew. The *real* Jim Sherwood loves you with all his heart."

"Maybe so, Ma. But . . . . I know one thing for sure: So help me God, I will *never* drink beer. And so help me God, I will *never* scream and swear at my wife and kids. And so help me God, I will *never* leave my wife alone night after night. I swear I won't be like my Pa."

Alice's expression of concern suddenly turned to wide-eyed horror. She covered her face with her hands and began to sob uncontrollably. Andrew put his arms around his mother and tried to comfort her.

"Ma? You're crying. What . . . what did I say to make you cry?"

Eventually, she was able to speak. "I . . . I know you mean it, Son—about not drinking and about not being cruel to your wife and children. But your Pa said the very same things—made the very same promises—even in the same tone of voice—twenty years ago . . . ."

Monday, January 18; lunch break *[18 days to competition]*

As the lunch break ended, Mr. Lesser approached Arlene Simmons, who had been sitting in the back of the band room, listening to the rehearsal while she ate her sack lunch.

"Miss Simmons? It's nice to see you again. Is there some reason you're not eating in the cafeteria today?" There was kindness in Mr. Lesser's voice.

"Sir? I know I was an awful fool to ditch rehearsal. I know that you had every right to kick me out of band. I . . . I guess I can't be in band, guess I can't be there to help Oregon City take State . . . . But . . . well, isn't there something I can do? Take charge of the sheet music for you? Maybe I could be the equipment manager? Maybe I could . . . ."

Very gently, Mr. Lesser replied. "Miss Simmons, You can't be part in and part out. When you chose to break the training rules, you chose to be out of the band."

Arlene was disappointed. "That's it, Sir?"

"That's it. You're welcome to visit rehearsals. You can eat your lunch here. Come as often as you like. But only as a guest and a friend—not as a member of the band."

"Yes, Sir. And Sir? If I can't be part of the band, I can still wish the band well. Good luck at the competition."

Was this Arlene Simmons talking? Mr. Lesser was intrigued.

"Arlene? You've changed. What has happened?"

"I guess . . . I guess I'm a little older and a little smarter, Mr. Lesser. All my life I've been able to get what I wanted by making my own rules and breaking everyone else's. And now I've learned, here in the band room, that some people have rules and really stick by them. And . . . and I guess I always wished it were so, even when I was breaking the rules myself.

"Mr. Lesser? It sounds strange, I guess, but I knew when I came in here today that you wouldn't let me back in the band. I knew you'd stick to your rules. I think I would have been disappointed if you hadn't stuck to your rules. I've decided I'd like to live my life with your kind of rules, instead of rules people make and then ignore."

9
The Tymps

Tuesday, January 19; late evening [17 days to competition]

It was very dark and very quiet in the band room. The only light was coming from the hallway under the band room door. Chairs and music stands stood where they had been left when the low brass sectional had ended an hour ago. There was not light enough to make out the training rules Carole Larsen had written on the blackboard six weeks ago, though a sharp pair of eyes might have made out the "No Exceptions" notation Mr. Lesser had added.

From out in the hallway came a sound of a man approaching the band room door. Then came the noise of a key in the lock, and of the double doors opening. Silhouetted against the hallway light stood Mr. Cochran, pushing two large boxes on a wheeled cart.

The Principal turned on the light and surveyed the slave quarters. Then he pushed his cart to the back of the room. A sly smile on his face, he unloaded the two large boxes. From his pocket he took a large black crayon, and wrote "OREGON CITY TAKE STATE!" on each box. Then he lifted the two ancient tymps onto the cart, and pushed the cart toward the door. Turning the lights off, Mr. Cochran again locked the doors to the band room.

Again all was dark in the band room, the only light coming from under the door. Again all was silent, except for the receding footsteps of a high school principal humming the main theme from Shostakovich's Fifth Symphony.

Wednesday, January 20; late evening [16 days to competition]

The Wednesday night percussion sectional was going well. There was no banter, no laughter, no distractions as Mr. Lesser sent his percussion section into the mud pits of Egypt to make bricks for Pharaoh.

"Good, People! But it's got to *build* as we near the end. We start at *fortissimo* and build to a crashing triple *fortissimo* at the end. Piano: More on the right hand. Mr. Arnold: Are you being polite to those new tymps? I want to *hear* it! Xylophone, your high notes will carry. You can play it a bit softer.

"Again, from seven bars before 'N'. Ready? Begin!" The percussion section worked through the music, no longer several individuals, but *one* sound, *one* section, *one* mind.

As they played, Wally Arnold's father approached the band room and opened the door. Entering, he stood and listened, obviously impressed. The music built to a thundering, crashing conclusion, with Wally hammering out the final four quarter notes on the tymps.

"Wow!" exclaimed Mr. Arnold. "That is just incredible!"

"Agreed," said Mr. Lesser. "I think the percussion section is ready to take State! That will do it for tonight, People. Good job! See you in the morning, as soon as the busses arrive."

Mr. Arnold and his son approached Mr. Lesser as the other band members were leaving. "I think you're going to do it! I think Oregon City is going to take State!"

Mr. Lesser responded softly. "Seven and a half weeks ago these kids thought they were losers. Look at them now: they're winners, one and all. They're winners, and they know it. I just can't believe how this band has blossomed!"

"Mr. Lesser, these kids have caught the imagination of the whole town. Is there something we parents can do to help? I'm a member of the J.C.'s . . . and Johnson's dad is in Kiwanis. I think Annie Thomas' dad is in the Elks Lodge. Is there something we could do to help?"

"Well . . . you're already helping by getting the kids to and from rehearsals and by encouraging them to practice."

"New instruments?"

"No . . . with the new tymps, we're pretty well set there."

"Uniforms?"

"Uniforms? Of course! If you could fix the kids up with new uniforms for the state competition . . . ."

"Done! Mr. Lesser, you take care of the music. The town will take care of the new uniforms! These kids are going to take State in style!"

Thursday, January 21; evening [15 days to competition]

A number of students were seated in booths at Burger Shack, having an evening snack. The door opened and four members of the brass section entered. A waitress brought glasses of water and took their orders.

Chuck spoke first. "I'm so *sick* of the Fifth Symphony! I'm sure I'll throw up if I ever hear it again!"

Lee agreed. "I hear it in my sleep!"

"Jeez!" Martin began. "It's Shostakovich before school. It's Shostakovich in First Period . . . ."

" . . . and at lunch," added Lee.

Junior mimicked Mr. Lesser: "Don't forget your practicing at home!"

Chuck continued the mimic bit. " . . . and listen to the record!"

Junior picked up on the game. " . . . and you need private lessons on Saturday . . . ."

" . . . and sectional rehearsals!"

"Hey, don't you wish sometimes that Shostakovich had been some great inventor?"

"Maybe a plumber."

"Or maybe stillborn!"

There was a pause. "Two weeks more of this! I'm afraid I'll go AWOL . . . ."

"Two weeks more of this, and they'll have to send my mail to the Nut Hut in Salem."

"And my lip to the hospital!"

"Now there's a topic folks. My upper lip feels like it's been jammed into a little metal lip-grinding machine for five hours a day for eight weeks!"

Junior added, "Sometimes I can see my poor lip as it comes out the bell of my tuba!"

"Folks, I'm about ready to run away and join the army. Maybe they'd send me to some lovely, far-away place where they've never heard of Dmitri Shostakovich."

"They'd send your butt to Korea . . . ."

" . . . where you'd get *shot!*"

"And then Saint Peter would send you and your miserable bugle straight to hell!"

"Right. And you'd spend all eternity playing . . . ."

"I know, I know: The Fifth Symphony."

Some football lettermen and their girl friends from another booth came over to join in this good-natured griping.

"Hey, it sounds like you guys are getting a little tired of training rules . . . ."

Junior shot back, "You got that one right!"

"Yeah, it gets old fast."

A football player spoke next: "Hey, do you guys really think you've got a shot at taking State?"

Martin replied for all of them. "You'd better believe it!" We are going to show those other schools where the bear went through the buckwheat!"

"That's right! We are, putting it modestly, simply the best band in the Great State of Oregon."

"Seriously, is that hot air, or is that for real?"

"Well . . . we've come a long way in eight weeks. I didn't know you could get so good at something by working hard at it. But Mr. Lesser says we've got a ways to go still."

The football player sounded more like a coach than a left tackle: "Then don't screw up like we did. It's the *last* part of training, the hard part when you're tired or bored or going nuts that makes the difference. See, that's when *we* let up. That's why we got beat."

"This guy sounds like Ervin Lesser," said Lee.

"Call it what you want," responded the football player. "Still it's true. I can't tell you how much I want to see *somebody* in this stinking high school win *something*. We're with you—all of us. If you guys don't take State, we'll pound on you . . . ."

One of the girls spoke up. "Hey! I've got an idea. We have pep rallies before football games, don't we? I think we ought to have a big bonfire and a pep-rally for the band! I'm going to talk to Sally and Ann . . . ."

The same night; late evening.

While there still was daylight, Andrew worked on the new fence. When it became too dark to build fence, he turned to his chores, milking the cows, feeding the chickens, cutting the firewood. As he worked, snatches of music from the Fifth Symphony ran through his mind.

After he had carried the day's firewood into the basement, Andrew knelt to put a couple of logs in the furnace. More tired than he had ever been in his life, he stopped working and leaned against the stacked wood. Instantly, he fell asleep.

A few minutes later Andrew's mother entered the basement and found her son asleep, kneeling beside the wood pile. "Andrew? Andrew, are you all right?"

Startled, Andrew awoke. "Ma? I guess I just . . . ."

"That's enough wood for tonight, Son. Come, let's have some dinner."

Still kneeling in the same place, Andrew closed his eyes again. "I'm kinda tired, Ma. Maybe . . . Maybe I'll just skip supper and go to bed . . . get up early tomorrow and . . . ." The boy was asleep again.

"You need to eat, Son. You've got to keep your strength up."

"Yeah, Ma. You go on up to the kitchen. I'll be up in a minute." Andrew's mother watched as her son fell asleep once more.

Alarmed, Alice Sherwood awakened the boy once more. "Let me help you, Son. Let's get you into your bed right now."

Friday, January 22; afternoon [14 days to competition]

Three popular female band members were in the restroom, checking their makeup and talking.

"About one more week of Shostakovich, and I'll have to say good-bye forever to Roy."

"Tell me about it. Roger says he wants a *girlfriend*, not just a picture of one."

"I guess I'm lucky. My sweetie has been pretty good about this whole thing, except he thinks I'm going steady with some guy named Dmitri."

At this moment Julie entered the restroom. The other girls looked at her and smiled.

"And speaking of lucky . . . how would it be to have your boyfriend in the *band*?"

There was a cattiness in the next voice: " . . . *and* have him assigned to sit next to you!"

"But what good is a boyfriend who blushes when he sees himself in the mirror?" All three girls snickered.

Julie, with fire in her eyes, whipped around to face the much shorter girls. For a split-second, one of them looked pleased to have gotten a response out of Julie. But the tables turned as Julie silently glared at each one of them individually, causing them to avert their eyes. Had Julie appeared embarrassed, they might have thought they had gotten the best of her. But it was obvious by the look on her face that Julie wasn't angry for her own sake, but because they had tried to cut down Andrew.

Suddenly appearing uncomfortable, the three girls turned around and headed for the door, leaving behind an unruffled Julie, who now appeared to stand five-foot-twenty-four.

Saturday, January 23; mid-day [13 days to competition]

It was Saturday, and another huge stump was being coaxed from its ancient place, one root at a time. Jim Sherwood and his son worked steadily, methodically, first digging around a root to expose it, then holding the root taut with the steel bar while chopping through it with the axe. Hour after hour of this slow, exhausting work passed.

At length Andrew sat down. His heart was pounding, and he was dizzy.

"Come on, Boy. You ain't tired yet?"

"Just a little, Pa."

"That's a crock! It's only just past lunch-time, and already you're tired?"

"I . . . I didn't get to sleep 'til late last night, Pa. Just let me rest for a minute, and I'll . . . ."

"Rest? Rest? That's all you *ever* do: Rest on your butt at school and suck on that stupid saxophone! What you got to be tired about? Never do a useful thing around here!"

"Pa . . . I . . . I'm a little winded . . . ."

"Winded? Too much band and not enough chores is how I read it. **Out** 'til all hours, gettin' home late, doin' half a job on your chores. And then making that awful saxophone racket half the night. What kind of a way is that to live?"

Andrew made no response.

"Crud! When I was your age, I knew how to *work!* Never thought I'd have a son who'd be ugly and stupid and lazy at the same time!"

"Pa . . . ."

"Shut your mouth! Now knock it off with the lame excuses and help me get this stump out of the ground!"

It was no good trying to reason with the Old Man. "Yes, Pa."

Andrew took the shovel and returned to the pit.

Monday, January 25; after school [11 days to competition]

With only a few minutes remaining in the hour, Mr. Lesser stopped the rehearsal to talk with the members of the band.

"We're getting there, People. But we've only got less than two weeks left before the competition, and I'm worried. I'm still hearing individual players instead of sections. Clarinets, flutes: you've *got* to clean up your thirty-second note runs in the *allegro*. Cornets, trumpets: you're not pulling together. Percussion: you set the tempo. Don't speed up just because we get louder. Some of you second and third-chair people *must* work harder. You've got to come up to first-chair execution."

Mr. Lesser took a deep breath, then let it out in a long sigh. "Frankly, People, if I were one of the judges, I couldn't give you a 'superior' right now."

"We've still got two weeks, Sir," said Wally, "and we're getting better every day . . . ."

"What we've got left is eight school days—and I don't think it's going to be enough. If we're going to take State, we're going to have to squeeze harder."

Chuck shrugged his shoulders. "Squeeze harder? What's left to squeeze, Sir?"

"We need . . . we need to practice here *every* night—all of us. We need to cancel all the sectionals and have a full band rehearsal every school night!"

A murmur ran through the band room. "Oh, no!" "Too much, that's too much." "I can't hack it."

Mr. Lesser spoke sharply. "Listen, People! I know it's asking a lot. It's an impossibility. It's insanity. I know all that. You're exhausted. You're sick of the music. You've got other classes, other interests. You've got families. You've got homework. You hate the sight of this room, this music, this conductor. I know all of that.

"And guess what! *I'm* sick of it, too. I'm sick nigh unto death of Shostakovich—and this room—and even you people sometimes." There was a long pause.

"But that doesn't help us get the job done, does it? Here are our choices: we can go on for the next several days as we have in the past, getting better and better—and we'll take an 'excellent' in the competition. We will be one of the best bands in the state.

"Or, we can pay the full price. We can climb in the pot and turn up the heat. We can bear down and *move* this thing from 'excellent' to 'superior' and be the one and only *best* band in this state.

"Now, what's it going to be?" Very quietly—almost in a whisper—Mr. Lesser said, "Anyone who can't take it had better get up and leave right now. There is no place for 'almost perfect' in the New York Philharmonic."

There was total silence in the band room. No one moved.

"That's it, then, People? All right. Then on top of all other rehearsals and practicing, there will be a two-hour rehearsal every school night until the competition a week from Friday. You miss once, you're out. No exceptions. Absolutely no exceptions for any reason unless you have a note from the hospital.

"Now, go home and get some dinner. I'll see *all* of you back here at seven."

Everyone left except Andrew. He stayed in his seat, practicing the bassoon part on his baritone sax. Julie left her instrument case to get her coat. While she was gone, Andrew opened the case and slipped a small, folded note inside.

By the time Julie returned, the two of them were alone in the room, with Mr. Lesser out of sight in the storage room. Bending down, Julie whispered "I think my Dad likes you, Andrew, but not as much as I do."

Andrew smiled shyly, then stammered, "I . . . I think . . . I think I like you, too, Julie."

"Andrew? How are you going to get home after these rehearsals? You can't just walk home seven miles every night."

"I . . . I'll be fine."

"Let me drive you home. I'm sure Daddy would let me have the car to drive you home."

"I . . . No . . . I mean . . . It's my load, and I've got to carry it . . . ."

"You're sure? I'd like to help you . . . ."

"I wish . . . I wish I . . . ." Thirty seconds passed before Andrew could finish his thought. "Julie? Thanks anyway."

After Julie left, Andrew considered his situation—and felt a wave of despair wash over him. "Dear God," he moaned, "a two-hour rehearsal *every* night. On top of everything else, a two-hour rehearsal every night! How do I sell *that* to the Old Man?"

Wednesday, January 27; evening [9 days to competition]

"Daddy, I'm worried."

Alton Ryckman put his newspaper down. "What are you worried about, Sis?"

"It's Andrew. Daddy, I just know that something is terribly wrong."

"What do you mean?"

"I think Andrew must be sick. Daddy, sometimes his hands just shake. And I know he must be losing weight. Sometimes he looks like he's so tired he's about to fall out of his chair."

"Probably nothing to worry about. Life on a farm is not easy—plus the band is taking a lot of his time right now. I'm sure Andrew will be all right. A lot of high school kids burn their candles on both ends."

"It's more than just tiredness, Daddy. There's a look in his face like . . . almost like a hunted animal. I'm really worried."

"When's the band competition? A week from Friday? That's only a few days, Sis. After that, the pressure will be off. He'll probably sleep in for a few days, and then be fine . . . ."

"Daddy?" There was a real intensity in Julie's face. "I don't think it's going to just go away. Carole's folks know the Sherwoods well. They say that Mr. Sherwood is a heavy drinker, that he just screams at Andrew sometimes—that he calls Andrew terrible names, and that he works him night and day."

Julie had her father's attention now. "Does he beat up on the boy?"

"Well, I . . . I don't think so. But . . . ."

Mr. Ryckman weighed his words before speaking. "Sis, I hate to say it, but short of calling the police, there's not much we can do. And anyway, I doubt that what Mr. Sherwood is doing is breaking any laws . . . ."

There was anger in Julie's response: "Isn't slavery against the law? Didn't Abraham Lincoln abolish slavery?"

"Slavery? Maybe you're overstating it a bit, Sis. Good hard work and fresh air are more likely to help Andrew than hurt him. You'll see, Sis. Andrew will be just fine when the competition's over."

10
The Bridge

***Friday, January 29; early morning** [7 days to competition]*

As Andrew returned to the porch with the milk buckets, his parents were at it again. As always, they were arguing about him.

"Well, for crying out loud, Woman, what do *you* think? Do *you* think it's normal to have a stupid saxophone take up your whole day?"

Andrew's mother was pleading. "It's only for one more week, Jim. One week from today is the competition . . . ."

"And that is one week too long! Why, the boy walks around like some zombie, he's so tired. He's doing half a job on his chores and half a job on his homework."

"He wouldn't be so tired if you didn't have him working like a slave to build that fence!"

"That fence is there to teach him a lesson!"

"What lesson? That he can never be with his friends? That he can never have a girlfriend? That he can never go to a dance?"

Outside on the porch Andrew heard all of this as he strained the milk and washed out the buckets. He entered the kitchen in the midst of World War III.

"I'll ask him myself," Jim roared. "Andrew, are you doing as well in school as you can do?"

"Probably not, Pa, but I . . . ."

"And are you getting your chores done on time?"

"Pa, I've got . . . ."

"And how many hours a day are you spending on this saxophone racket?"

"I . . . I don't know, Pa . . . ."

"Try this question: When was the last time you cleaned out the barn? I'll bet you jolly-well can't recall the last time!"

"I . . . ."

"No, No, and No once again! This is all wrong and upside down. *School* is important. *Chores* are important. *Work* is important. And that idiot band music is *not* important!"

Andrew's mother could see a disaster in the making, and was working frantically to prevent it. "Jim! Jim Sherwood, listen to me. It's only for one more week. One more week!"

"No! My mind is made up! This music crap is coming to a great big screeching, grinding halt!"

Andrew spoke up, pleading. "Pa, there is no way I can leave the band now. They—all of them—they're counting on me. I've got a part that nobody else can play . . . ."

"Bull!"

"Pa . . . . I promised you I'd get my work done and keep my grades up. Pa, I've kept my promise . . . ."

"Bull!"

"Jim! You promised this boy . . . ."

"I don't care *what* I promised. I know what's best, and I will decide. It's over! Finished! The boy is out of the band! And I mean right *now*!"

Furious, Jim Sherwood picked up his lunch bucket and left, slamming the door on his way out to the pickup. Soon the vehicle was tearing down the driveway.

There was silence in the kitchen for a time as Andrew and his mother considered what had just happened. Each realized that somehow Andrew *had* to continue in band for at least another week. And each realized that going against Jim Sherwood's will would result in Andrew having to build a fence around the whole State of Oregon.

"Darned if you do, and darned if you don't," Andrew whispered.

"Maybe if Mr. Lesser talked with your Pa," his mother suggested. "Maybe he could make him see . . . ."

Andrew slumped into a chair at the table, his head in his hands. He felt as though he had been holding up a heavy load for far too long—and that the load had suddenly doubled in weight.

And then the unthinkable happened: the school bus rolled past the Sherwood home.

"The bus!" Alice shouted. "Oh, Andrew, there goes the bus!"

"Oh, good heavens!" Andrew snatched up the heavy baritone sax case and raced out of the house. Maybe—just maybe—he could get to the bus stop before the bus left. Without coat, without books, Andrew ran down the driveway in a speed born of sheer desperation. It was all very clear, all very logical in his mind: "If I miss the bus, I miss a rehearsal. And if I miss even one rehearsal, I'm out of the band."

Then came another anguished thought: "Pa says I'm out of band anyway. I've *got* to get to Mr. Lesser. Maybe Mr. Lesser can make Pa change his mind."

Andrew's long legs covered the hundred-yard driveway in seconds. He turned down the hill on Ferguson Road, raced to the bend in the road, around the bend toward the bus stop at the Walker Road junction. There! The bus was still there, just starting to move. "Surely someone will see me through the back window! Surely the driver will see me in his rear-view mirror. Surely . . . ."

The bus continued rolling, and disappeared from sight.

"The next stop! He'll stop at Copleys!" Andrew continued racing down the hill, hoping against hope that somehow he could board the bus at Copleys. The cold, wet air tore at Andrew's lungs as he continued running furiously down the steep hill. He rounded another turn, praying to see students boarding a yellow school bus.

What he saw was a bus already rolling, already pulling away from Copleys. Completely out of breath, Andrew stumbled to a stop, and watched the distant bus disappear from view.

Too late! Dear God in Heaven, too late, too late, too late! Andrew fell to his knees in the center of the gravel road, threw back his head, and emitted one long, unearthly scream in an agony of frustration—the scream of a soul without hope.

Same day; 9:00 a.m.

Distraught, disheveled, his clothing soaked through by the morning's rain and an almost seven-mile run, Andrew appeared in Mr. Lesser's office. He found the band leader at his desk, updating his grade book.

"Sir? I . . . I got here as soon as I could. I . . . I finally got a ride, Sir."

Mr. Lesser said nothing. He did not even look up from his desk at the boy standing behind him.

"Sir? I . . . I missed the bus. I wouldn't miss a rehearsal for anything, Sir. My Pa, he . . . ."

Still Mr. Lesser said nothing.

"Sir? I thought maybe you could talk with my Pa, and . . . ."

Mr. Lesser's voice was very quiet. "You broke the training rules, Mr. Sherwood. Leave the baritone sax in the storage room. I'll transfer you to First Period study hall."

"Sir?"

"Please close the door as you leave."

Andrew, still behind the band director, stood for a long time, seemingly unable to grasp what was happening. After a long time he whispered, "Yes, Sir." The soft click of the closing door latch sounded very much like something snapping.

Shoulders slumped, completely broken, Andrew left the baritone sax in the equipment room and picked up the tenor sax case. Slowly, he walked out of the band room. In the hallway he was greeted by the school's custodian, but answered the man not a word. The custodian watched Andrew leave the building and walk away from school into a light rain.

Andrew walked slowly, seemingly without purpose or destination toward 7th Street and lower Oregon City. At the bluff, he slowly descended the steep stone steps hugging the cliff side. Then he wandered west toward the river.

Walking out onto the old concrete bridge which spans the Willamette River and connects Oregon City with West Linn, Andrew paused for a moment to look with unseeing eyes at the dark, swirling water far below him. Then he approached the southeast tower—one of four which supported the arching span. Coatless, soaked to the skin, exhausted, Andrew shivered in the cold January air.

In the tower Andrew found the steel door which gave access to the bridge tower—a door which was supposed to be locked. Andrew tried the handle, and found the door open. He stepped inside, and pulled the door shut behind him. Absently, he threw the lock switch. Inside the dark tower, the shivering boy found a shelter of sorts in a mostly-enclosed "room." Pigeons entered and left via an uncovered air vent inaccessible to humans.

Still in a trance, Andrew took the tenor sax out of its case and mechanically assembled the instrument. Then he sat on the instrument case and began to play slow, moody songs without words—songs of despair. From the low register moaned the throaty anguish of hopelessness. Occasionally, the high register uttered a black cry of protest against . . . everything.

Andrew's tenor sax soliloquy alternately whispered and then screamed. The music asked questions for which there were no answers. It sued for peace and found none. It spoke of a hurt that wouldn't stop hurting. The music said all the things that a boy driven over the edge couldn't say.

Andrew heard none of the music he played. Occasionally he would stop, and a fleeting, puzzled look would cross his face, followed by an almost imperceptible, weary shaking of his head. Then he would resume the moody, hopeless music.

Outside, people in cars crossed the Willamette River Bridge, never hearing the musical cry of despair coming from the southeast tower.

The Same Day; afternoon

Andrew's mother was terribly worried. With no means of transportation and no telephone, she had sat at home all day, wondering whether Andrew had caught the bus or not, wondering if Mr. Lesser had agreed to reason with Jim, wondering if Andrew was all right.

She had determined to flag down the school bus and ask some questions. "Mr. Grant, I'm sorry to stop you like this, but . . . well, I'm worried about Andrew. Did he ride in to school with you this morning?"

"Why, no, I don't recall that he did. Hey, any of you kids know for sure if Andrew was on the bus this morning?"

The answer confirmed Alice Sherwood's worst fears.

"He wasn't in algebra, either," one girl volunteered.

"And I didn't see him in English," said another.

"I don't think I saw him at school all day," responded a third.

The bus driver could see the concern on Mrs. Sherwood's face. "Is there something I can do?" he asked.

"I've got to get to town," Alice Sherwood replied. "May I ride in with you?"

The same day; about 4:30 p.m.

An emergency meeting was in progress in Mr. Cochran's office. Mr. Cochran and Mr. Lesser were speaking with the chief of Oregon City's small police force.

"Tom, we're not talking here about some kid who's a trouble-maker. Other kids might ditch classes or run away from home, but not this boy. This kid's a straight-A student."

"I just know something is wrong," Andrew's mother said. "There was a terrible scene at home this morning—an awful argument. Andrew's father told the boy he had to give up band . . . and Andrew was going to appeal to Mr. Lesser to talk to my husband, to try to reason with him. Then the school bus went past, and Andrew started running to catch the bus, and . . . ."

Mr. Lesser was starting to see the whole picture for the first time—starting to see that he had turned his back on Andrew at the very time when the boy most desperately needed him. "He's a fine boy, Mrs. Sherwood. I'm sure he's all right."

"That's right," the police chief said. "We'll find him. Try not to worry."

The telephone in the office rang, and Mrs. Brandon answered it. "Yes, Mr. Copley? Thanks for calling back. Yes. Yes. I see. Well, thank you for trying. Yes. Good-bye, and thanks again." Mrs. Brandon didn't have to tell anyone in the office that Andrew still was not at home.

"Where is the boy's father?" the police chief asked Mrs. Sherwood.

"He works in Portland as a carpenter," she replied. "Before going home, he often stops at the Coney Island Bar to have a few beers."

"Mrs. Brandon," the chief said, "Would you call Coney Island for me? Leave word for the boy's father to call the police station."

The custodian, Mr. Schwartz, entered the office and began emptying waste baskets. Overhearing the discussion in progress, he asked, "Andrew Sherwood? Tall, muscular kid? Maybe I can help. About nine this morning I saw him walking down the hall with a case of some kind in his hand—a musical instrument, I guess. I spoke to him, but he just sort of looked right through me. Didn't say a word. He walked right out the door and into the rain. I thought it was kind of strange, so I watched him for a minute. He was walking very slowly toward lower Oregon City."

Same Day; about 5:00 p.m.

The streets were wet, but the rain had stopped. At five o'clock the whistle blew at the Crown-Zellerbach paper plant in West Linn. A large number of workers, some in cars, some on foot, left the plant and walked toward the Willamette River Bridge. Traffic was very slow—frequently at a dead stop—as cars waited for the traffic light on the Oregon City end of the old bridge to change.

Several pedestrians walking across the bridge heard music coming from the southeast tower. Some stopped to listen and comment, then walked on. One man, lunch bucket in hand, searched out the source of

the music, then tried the handle on the steel door. Finding the door locked, he knocked—
softly at first, then louder.

"Is everything all right?" he called out. "Who's in there?"

The moody blues music continued without interruption. A puzzled look on his face, the pedestrian then walked briskly away from the tower to the pay phone at the end of the bridge.

Inserting a nickel, the pedestrian dialed "0", and said, "Operator? Would you connect me with the police?"

Same Day; about 6:00 p.m.

Traffic on the bridge had been closed, and policemen were rerouting traffic. Near the southeast tower were Mr. Lesser's car plus two police vehicles, their emergency lights flashing eerily in the darkness. Policemen stood at each end of the bridge to turn away the gawkers and the rubber-neckers.

One after another the little group of people on the bridge took their turns knocking on the locked steel door and calling out to the musician in-side the tower. For an answer they received only a beautiful tenor sax requiem, a dirge of hopelessness.

"Andrew? This is Mr. Lesser. Can you hear me? I was wrong this morning, not hearing the whole story before I acted. Please open the door so we can talk. I want to make things right."

Alice Sherwood was near hysteria. "Jim has driven that boy like a plow mule. He's cursed him, belittled him, called him terrible names. He's piled work on top of work, and with never a word of thanks. He's worn him down physically and now he's broken his mind."

"I could see that the boy was tired," Mr. Lesser observed, "but I had no idea he was getting that kind of pressure at home. I've loaded him down at school when he was already overloaded at home."

Mr. Cochran tried. "Andrew? This is the principal. We're here to help you. No one wants to hurt you. Whatever the problems are, we can work them out. Please unlock the door. We can't help you until you unlock the door."

It was as though the cold, wet, shivering boy inside the dark tower could not hear. The beautiful blues music continued to cry out from a tenor sax in pain.

The chief of police proposed direct action. "I'll have the fire department bring in an acetylene torch. We can burn the hinges off that steel door in a couple of minutes."

"Not yet," counseled the principal. "Let's avoid the acetylene torch if we can, since we don't know the boy's state of mind. We just don't know what he might do."

Mr. Cochran's own words gave him an idea. "Chief, can you patch us through on your radio to the hospital? There's a doctor there—I think his name is Feldman—who is a psychiatrist. Maybe he could help us."

"Jerry Feldman?" asked Mr. Lesser. "Dr. Jerome Feldman? His daughter, Laurie, is in the band."

"So much the better," said Mr. Cochran. Then the police chief handed him the car radio's speaker.

While the little group on the bridge waited for Dr. Feldman, Alice Sher-wood leaned against the steel door, her face on the wet metal. "Andrew? Can you hear me, Son? This is your mother. Son, I've let you down, and I know it." Mrs. Sherwood's words were distorted by the tightness in her throat, and punctuated by her sobs. "I've stood aside when I should have spoken up. I've watched you being abused and didn't do nearly enough to stop it . . . . Son? Can you hear me?"

Being careful that Mrs. Sherwood not hear him, the police chief said to Mr. Lesser and Mr. Cochran, "I've got a bad feeling about all of this. I'm going to radio the hospital to send down an ambulance, too."

The Chief turned to a sergeant nearby, "Moulton, I want you to get inside one of the other bridge towers. See what we've got. See if there are any other ways in or out. See what sort of structure we've got behind these steel doors. Wood? steel? enclosed? open? See if the boy is safe, or if he's in a place where he might fall through into the river. Get back to me as soon as you have something to report!"

Within minutes Dr. Feldman pulled his car to a stop near the others on the bridge. The principal and Mr. Lesser spent a few minutes telling him what Mrs. Sherwood had told them. All the while, the beautiful, sad music continued from the tower.

"Let me see what we've got," said Dr. Feldman. "Mistreated by an abusive father; overworked at home; overworked at school; physically exhausted. One major crisis at home this morning followed by another at school. Then seen walking away from school in a trance . . . ."

" . . . plus cold and wet and hungry," added Mrs. Sherwood.

The police chief asked impatiently, "Doctor, why won't he talk to us? Why won't he open the door? Why does he keep playing that music?"

"I'm not sure yet, Chief," responded the doctor. "Let me see what I can do to find out." He stepped to the steel door and went to work.

"Andrew? Andrew, can you hear me?" asked the Doctor. The mournful music continued.

"Andrew? This is Doctor Feldman from the hospital. I'm Laurie's dad. If you can hear me, please stop playing for a moment." The music continued without a break.

"Andrew? Can I get you a coat? Can I get you something to eat?" No response, except for more music.

"Dr. Feldman, it's as if the boy is not hearing anything we say," said Mr. Cochran.

"I think you're right," said the doctor. "A person under great pressure may come to a point where his mind can't cope with people any more."

From the end of the bridge there came a loud commotion. Soon **Jim** Sherwood's pickup screeched to a stop beside the other cars on **the** bridge. He walked straight to his wife. "Alice, what is going on here?"

"Jim, it's Andrew," she said, grief in her face. "After you told him he couldn't be in the band, he . . . ."

"He what?" demanded Jim.

"He ran to school," replied Mr. Lesser. "I guess he wanted me to talk with you . . . persuade you to let him continue with band."

"Well you had better not have told him he could do it!" shouted Jim.

"I didn't," said Mr. Lesser quietly. "I kicked him out of band for missing a rehearsal."

Jim turned to his wife. "So where is the blockhead now?"

"He's . . . Andrew's locked inside the bridge tower," said Alice, pointing at the steel door. "He's playing music, but he won't talk to anyone."

"Well, you see if I don't put a stop to *that* right now!" he shouted as he walked to the steel door.

"Andrew?" he shouted, pounding on the steel door with his fists. "This is your Pa. Now stop this foolishness and get your lazy butt out here where I can kick it!"

The moody music continued unchanged.

"Listen to me, Bonehead!" shouted Jim. "You're embarrassing me in front of all these people! Now put that damnable saxophone down and unlock this door!"

"It won't work," said Dr. Feldman, trying to be soothing. "Mr. Sherwood, it won't work because the boy can't hear you."

"What do you mean he can't hear me?" he shouted, a look of rage on his face.

"Exactly that," repeated Dr. Feldman. "Your boy can't hear a thing you or I or anyone else says. His mind has just shut down for a while."

"That's a crock!" yelled Jim. "I don't believe that head-doctor crap!" With that, Jim strode to his pickup and pulled out a sledgehammer. "We'll see if that *lock* can hear what I have to say!"

Dr. Feldman put a hand on Jim Sherwood's arm and looked directly into his eyes. "Mr. Sherwood? It really is true: your son is terribly sick right now. Banging on that steel door with a hammer will only make things worse. And that's not 'head-doctor crap.' That's the truth."

A puzzled, worried expression crossed Jim Sherwood's face. "I don't understand," he said, suddenly very quiet. "What is going on here?"

"Mr. Sherwood, I wish I knew. Better yet, I wish I knew what to do about it."

Sergeant Moulton was back with his report. "Chief? I forced the lock on the northeast tower. Inside the tower is sort of an open room with old two-by-twelve boards for flooring, supported on the ends by the steel bridge structure. It looks like the rooms were intended for storage of some kind.

"Unless you are a pigeon, there is just no way a person could get in or out without going through the steel door. And Chief? I hate to say it, but it's wet and moldy inside there, and those boards have been there for a long time. Plus, there's been some vandalism, at least in the northeast tower. I'm not sure how much that old flooring will hold. If that flooring goes, the boy drops right into the Willamette."

The Chief appeared worried. "Dr. Feldman, what about taking the hinges off that door with a torch? It wouldn't take but a couple of minutes."

"Chief, it may well come to that . . . but not yet. We simply don't know enough about the boy's state of mind to chance it just yet. About all we know so far is that he can't seem to hear human voices."

That gave Mr. Lesser an idea. "Well, if he can't hear *voices*, maybe . . . maybe he could hear something else." The band leader stepped to his car and opened the trunk, from which he removed his trumpet case. Fitting the mouthpiece to the horn, Mr. Lesser returned to the tower door and began to slowly play the main theme from the Fifth Symphony.

After a few bars, he stopped to listen. Silence. For the first time, the moody saxophone music had stopped. "Andrew," he called. "Can you hear me? Open the door, Andrew." Nothing. And then the woeful saxophone music began anew.

Again Mr. Lesser played the main theme on his trumpet. And this time the tenor saxophone inside the tower joined him!

"That's progress!" observed Dr. Feldman with excitement. "Mr. Lesser, maybe you've found a bridge—a way to communicate with the boy." The doctor knocked on the steel door and called out, "Andrew? Can you hear me now? Please come out. You can't stay here on the bridge all night."

For a response, Dr. Feldman got only silence. Then the mournful blues music began again, only slower this time.

"Talking doesn't get us a thing," mused Mr. Lesser, his brow furrowed with worry and concentration. "The only way we communicate at all is when my trumpet speaks to his sax. All we've got tonight is Dmitri Shostakovich."

Mr. Lesser looked at his watch, then turned to the police chief. "Chief? Can you get a couple of cars up to the high school on the double? Tell the kids in the band room that we've got a problem. Send them all home except the section leaders. Bring the section leaders with you, and have them bring their instruments. Oh, and be sure to bring the baritone sax from the storage room."

"I'll have our dispatcher send two cars code three," the chief responded, stepping to his police car radio to give the orders.

Mr. Lesser turned to the principal. "Mr. Cochran, why don't you go, too? Take my car. You can brief the band members on what we've got here, and then bring a carload of section leaders back with you."

Ten minutes later two police cars arrived, together with several student vehicles and Mr. Cochran. But out of the cars poured not just section leaders, but the entire band, many with instruments. Out of one car stepped a newspaper editor and his terribly worried daughter.

"People," Mr. Lesser said to his band, "We are about to hold the most important rehearsal of our lives. We've got a very sick boy—a friend of ours—behind that locked steel door. We're not sure how long the wooden floor in there will support him.

"He's wet and cold, and he hasn't eaten in twenty-four hours. He's more tired than any of us ever have been. He's come to where his mind can't—or won't—listen to people any more. I guess too many people have hurt him too many times . . . and I've been one of those who has hurt him the most.

"Andrew doesn't seem to be hearing voices. It seems that the only thing that can get through to him tonight is music. Now gather 'round in a tight circle, and let's try to help our friend."

"Mr. Swinton, have you got that baritone sax put together? I hope and pray we're going to need it in a few minutes. Now, from Letter 'I', People. The bassoon solo, and loud enough so that our friend inside that tower can hear it. Ready? Begin!"

The music began, eerie music made more eerie by the time and the place and the flashing lights of the police cars and the ambulance—music made urgent by the desperate need for it to be heard by an audience of one.

A wave of relief ran through the entire band as they realized they were hearing music from inside the tower. A tenor saxophone was playing the bassoon solo!

Speaking loudly so Andrew could hear, Mr. Lesser called, "Cut! Good, People! That sounds really good. But there's something wrong here." In a louder voice he said, "Mr. Sherwood, you've got the bassoon part. You can't play the bassoon part on a tenor sax. Mr. Swinton, would you take the baritone sax over to the door so Mr. Sherwood can get it?"

"Yes, Sir," he said, starting toward the door. But Barry was stopped by a tall, slender, terribly worried oboe player.

She turned to Mr. Lesser. "Sir? May I?" Then she took the baritone sax, and walked to the steel door. "Andrew?" she called. "I'm . . . I'm right here.

Andrew? It's Julie. I . . . I can't get the door open, Andrew. Won't you please help me with the door?"

The traffic light at the Oregon City end of the bridge changed, while on the bridge there was absolute silence. Every eye watched to see if the steel door would open. Nearly a full minute passed before the sound of a lock was heard, followed by the creaking of a steel door turning on seldom-used hinges.

Andrew emerged from the tower door, a puzzled look on his face. The tenor sax in one hand, he said not a word as he reached for the baritone in Julie's hands.

"Oh Andrew! Andrew!" Julie cried over and over, embracing the tall boy fiercely. Her face buried in Andrew's neck, she wept openly. Gently, Mr. Cochran took one instrument from Andrew as Mr. Lesser took the other.

Nearly overcome with relief, Andrew's mother joined Julie in embracing the boy. Confused, still not understanding, Jim Sherwood stood to one side, watching, wondering, fearing.

Andrew, a distant, vacant look on his face, gently disengaged himself from everyone, then turned to Mr. Lesser. In a voice completely devoid of emotion, barely audible, he said, "You were wrong, Sir. I *wanted* it. I worked hard for it—worked harder than anybody else. I paid the full price." There was a very long pause before he concluded. "But you were wrong, Sir. No matter how much I gave, it was never enough."

Then he turned to his father. "And *you* were wrong, too, Pa. I got up early and I stayed up late and I really did learn to work. I worked until my body hurt all over. I did all my chores. I worked on your fence. But it wasn't enough . . . it was never enough . . . ." With those words, Andrew's eyes rolled up, and his knees buckled.

Jim Sherwood stepped forward and caught his son, then held the unconscious boy in his arms and sobbed "Dear God! What has happened to my boy?" Doctor Feldman and Mr. Lesser moved quickly to help Jim Sherwood support the unconscious boy.

"Chief," Doctor Feldman said urgently, "Can you give us a police escort for the ambulance? We need to get this boy to the hospital right away!"

11
The Hospital

Same Day; late at night

In the small waiting area near the emergency room of Oregon City Hospital sat Andrew's parents plus Mr. Cochran, Mr. Lesser, and Julie Ryckman.

"It's all right, Mama," said Jim Sherwood. "He's going to be fine." He sounded as though he were mostly trying to convince himself.

"I wish I could believe it, Jim . . . . But he looked so . . . so . . . ."

"Yes. As though his mind were a thousand miles away . . . ."

"And he was just shaking all over with the cold."

Now somewhat realizing that he himself must be partly responsible for what had happened to Andrew, Jim said softly, "Dear God in Heaven, what have I done to my boy?"

"And what have *I* done?" asked Ervin Lesser. "I'll never forgive myself if . . . ."

Mr. Cochran tried to reassure everyone. "I'm sure there's plenty of blame to go around, folks. But right now the important thing is not blame, it's that boy in there."

For the first time Julie spoke. "Mr. Cochran, I still don't understand. What happened to Andrew today?"

"No one can be sure yet, Julie. But this morning a boy who already was physically exhausted experienced an emotional catastrophe at home. Then he ran nearly seven miles in the rain so he could have another emotional catastrophe at school. I guess it was just more than his mind could handle."

" . . . and his mind . . . just . . . ?"

"I guess his mind just . . . shut down in self-defense."

"Shut down? You mean maybe we'll never . . . ?" There was grave concern on the girl's pretty face.

"Doctor Feldman should be able to give us a better answer. But Andrew is young and strong and I think there's a good chance he'll be all right."

Andrew's mother spoke for everyone in the room: "Oh, God, please let it be so!"

And Julie repeated the words. "Yes, dear God. Please let it be so."

Andrew's mother, hearing Julie repeat her plea, seemed to realize for the first time that the girl was present; that this girl was the Julie in the photograph which Andrew had showed her, and that she was someone very important in her son's life. The older woman took a seat next to the girl, put her arms around her, and said very gently, "Hello, Dear. I'm Andrew's mother. It's 'Julie,' isn't it? I'm so very glad there is a 'Julie' for my son."

Doctor Feldman entered the room, a serious expression on his face. Everyone rose, and gathered around him.

"Mr. and Mrs. Sherwood, I'm not yet exactly sure what we've got here. Clearly, your son is exhausted. I don't recall ever having seen a youngster so physically drained as this boy seems to be. He's suffering from exposure, of course, the sort of thing which might yet develop into pneumonia.

"All of that we can diagnose and treat. But it's clear enough that the boy also has experienced a severe emotional break, and that will be a good deal harder to deal with.

"Doctor Ahrens is with Andrew now. He's a medical doctor, and a good one. He's started Andrew on an I.V. to provide nourishment, and has given him a sedative. He'll be monitoring the boy closely throughout the night. For now, we've done all we can do."

Jim Sherwood spoke. "When will we be able to see him?"

"Well, we'd want him to sleep as long as possible, of course. And then when he awakens—assuming he does awaken—Doctor Ahrens and I will be examining him closely."

"Will it be all right if we visit him tomorrow? Sit in his room while we wait for him to . . . ."

"That will be fine. You understand, of course, that we have no way of knowing how long it may be before he comes out of this, whatever it is . . . ."

"Dr. Feldman?" It was Andrew's mother. "Is he going to . . . ?"

"It's too early to tell much, Mrs. Sherwood."

Jim spoke very quietly. "Doctor? Please take good care of my boy."

"We will, Mr. Sherwood. Now, you folks go on home and try to get some rest."

"Yes. Some rest. And I've got some chores to take care of." The little group moved toward the door and the cold night air.

The Same Day; late evening

Julie got out of the car and thanked both Mr. Lesser and Mr. Cochran for the ride. She hurried across the street, then entered the door of a small building with the words *Oregon City Enterprise* on the glass windows. Grateful for the warmth in the room, she removed her coat and walked to the desk where her father sat alone, typing with one finger of each hand.

Alton Ryckman rose to meet his daughter and to comfort her. Worried, he said quietly, "Hi, Sis. How's our boy?"

"Oh, Daddy," she said tearfully as she held out her arms to hug her father."

"It's going to be all right, Baby, I promise. You know, young people have such resilience—I just know he'll snap back and be fine."

"That's what everybody says." Julie sounded unconvinced.

"You've got to have faith, Sis. All things are possible to those who believe."

Julie pulled back slightly from her father's embrace. She looked into the eyes of the editor of the newspaper and said, "Daddy? how will *The Enterprise* report all of this?"

"Sis, I have a responsibility to report the news . . . ."

Julie brushed past the editor, and picked up several pages of double-spaced typed copy. She read the headline aloud: HIGH DRAMA ON THE BRIDGE. Skimming the first couple of paragraphs, she looked up, anger on her face. "Daddy! You *can't* run this! Hasn't Andrew suffered enough already without *this?*"

"I'm a newspaper man, Sis. My job is to report the news."

"You're also a human being, a father, a Christian!"

Mr. Ryckman's stern face softened. He turned and pulled a sheet of paper from his typewriter, then handed his last draft to Julie. "Bingo, Sis." Tearing up the first story, he said, "*This* was written by a newspaper man.

"*That*", he said, pointing to the draft in her hands, was written by your Daddy."

Julie's expression softened. She spoke with relieved exasperation: "I might have known! Sometimes I don't know what to do with you, Daddy."

Mr. Ryckman put on his coat and walked with his daughter toward the door of the *Enterprise* Building. He turned off the light and locked the door. After he and Julie were in the car and driving up the hill toward home, he made a suggestion.

"You ought to shoot me."

"Hmmm?"

"You said you didn't know what to do with me, and I'm suggesting that you ought to shoot me."

"Daddy, what *are* you talking about?"

"One night last week you told me how worried you were about Andrew's health. Remember? You told me how badly he was being treated at home, how close to exhaustion he was. You told me enough that I should have seen what was coming.

"But I didn't see it, or I didn't want to see it. Maybe if I had acted then . . . ." There was a very long pause before Alton Ryckman pronounced sentence on himself. "I'm as much to blame as anyone else that that boy went over the edge."

Saturday, January 30; morning.

As soon as Doctor Feldman arrived at the hospital, he checked Andrew's chart and visited with the night nurse regarding the boy's condition. Then he stepped into Room 127 where he found Mr. and Mrs. Sherwood talking quietly as their son remained unconscious a few feet away.

"Good morning, Folks. No change so far, I guess."

"What . . . what do we do now, Doctor?"

"We wait. Soon Doctor Ahrens will be here to conduct some physical tests. My part of the program really begins when your son finally comes to."

"So you don't know yet if he . . . ?"

"Not yet. Say, have you folks had breakfast yet?"

"Yes, Sir. We ate at home right after the morning chores."

"I guess I need a cup of coffee and a donut. Mrs. Sherwood, why don't you wait here in Andrew's room. And Mr. Sherwood? Perhaps you'd like to join me for a cup of coffee?"

In the hospital lounge, Dr. Feldman poured a cup of coffee for himself and another for Jim, then found a pair of upholstered chairs.

"Mr. Sherwood?"

"Most folks call me 'Jim.'"

"Jim, I hope you'll not mind my asking you some rather personal questions . . . ."

Jim was immediately on the defensive: "You think I've been cruel to my son, don't you?"

"I think you've tried very hard to be a good father."

"Look, Doc, don't play head games with me. You saw how I acted on the bridge. You heard how I talked to my boy."

"I think what I saw was a man doing the best he could for a son he loves."

Jim looked for a long time at the doctor. "You . . . you don't think I'm some kind of a criminal who ought to be locked up?"

"Jim, let me ask you a question. Did your own father ever yell at you? Beat you up?"

"I don't remember my Pa."

"Your mother. Did she mistreat you?"

"No. I don't think my Ma ever raised her voice at me."

"Then *who*, Jim? I'd bet the rent money that you were mistreated as a child."

There was a long silence as Jim Sherwood pondered how this "head doctor" could know such a thing. Then he answered. "My step-dad."

"Your stepfather mistreated you?"

"My own Pa died when I was three. A few years later Ma married again —an older man, Charlie, who had never been around kids much . . . ."

"Did he yell at you sometimes? Strike you?"

For a long moment Jim eyed the doctor warily. Then he answered with anger. "Yeah! Yeah, Charlie yelled. He ranted and he raved and he screamed. And he beat up my Ma when I was too little to stop him. And he whipped me and my little sister with his belt. And at Christmas-time he . . . ." The rage in his voice turned almost into a sob as he trailed off.

Dr. Feldman spoke very quietly. "Jim, I want you to tell me all about it. Every rotten thing Charlie said. Every vicious thing he did. I want to hear all of it, and in minute detail. Tell me what he did to you and to your mother and to your sister. Tell me about Christmas with Charlie."

Jim was wary. "What for? What do you care if a dirty old man named Charlie Catton beat up his wife and step-kids thirty years ago? The old coot is dead now."

"I care because I want to help Andrew, and I want to help *you*. Jim, as near as I can figure it, I've got *two*—maybe three—abused boys here. *You* are every bit as much a victim as your son is. And before Andrew can have a chance at a decent life, we've got to get all of this anger and hurt and poison out of you. *You've* got to heal before you can help your son heal."

Jim looked at the doctor for a long, long time before answering with a question. "You think it really will help?"

"Jim, I *know* it will help. I think when we get done here, you'll see why you act the way you do, why you talk the way you talk. I think you'll stop shouting at Andrew. I think you'll be more loving with your wife. I think you'll drink a lot less. Because when we get done, Jim—once all of this is out in the open where we can talk about it and understand it—you'll like yourself a lot better. And I think you'll be able to forgive Charlie . . . ."

"Forgive *Charlie!*" Jim exploded. "Well, why in the name of all that is holy would I *ever* forgive that dirty old . . . ?"

"Because Charlie was a little boy once, Jim. Can you really hate a little boy named Charlie who is hurt and crying—and has just been beaten up by *his* father? You see, these things go from generation to generation. Who knows about Charlie's father and grandfather. It's a family sickness."

It turned out to be a very long cup of coffee for Dr. Feldman and for Jim.

The same day; noon

A nurse approached Dr. Ahrens. "Doctor? The Sherwood boy seems to be getting close to consciousness."

"Thank you, Nurse." The doctor stepped to a hall telephone and dialed the number of the lounge telephone. "Dr. Feldman? Yes. Yes. He seems to be rousing. Bring the boy's father, and I'll meet you in Room 127."

When Jim and the psychiatrist arrived, they found Dr. Ahrens studying the patient's chart. Seated in the room were Alice Sherwood and Julie, intently watching Andrew.

Andrew was lying on his back, perfectly still, but with his eyes open. Dr. Ahrens checked the boy's pulse, then applied a stethoscope to Andrew's chest. Next he examined the boy's eyes.

"Andrew?" The psychiatrist was the first to speak. "I'm Dr. Feldman. Doctor Ahrens and I are here to help you." Andrew, apparently still seeing and hearing nothing, slowly closed his eyes and returned to his deep sleep.

The two doctors looked at each other, puzzled. Then they took Andrew's parents and Julie into the hallway where they could talk openly. "Physically, he's rallying nicely. All vital signs look good. There are no indications of pneumonia. It's remarkable what fifteen hours of sleep have done for him physically . . . ."

Dr. Feldman observed wryly: "Looks like he's going back for more. Lynn, he's certainly not sleeping just because his body needs the rest—though certainly he's had a lot of catching up to do. Probably his mind is not yet ready to face reality. For weeks this boy has lived with ever-increasing physical and emotional pressure. As he lays there right now, Andrew is convinced that he has failed—that he has let the band down, that he has let Julie down, that everything important in his life is gone. He's convinced that he is powerless to control his own destiny. Why would he *want* to wake up?"

"So, where do we go from here, Jerry?"

"I'd continue the I.V. and let him sleep as long as he likes. The more he recovers physically, the better able his mind will be later to face the reality he's avoiding now. When he regains consciousness—and I'm sure he *will*— we'll try to show him that he has nothing to fear from reality . . . that he *does* have a say in the important decisions in his life . . . ."

"I agree. Thanks, Doctor. I'll be in touch if anything changes." Dr. Ahrens left.

After lunch, Dr. Feldman took Jim back to the hospital lounge for another "cup of coffee." Alice and Julie returned to Room 127 to watch and wait and be near Andrew.

Julie spoke first: "Mrs. Sherwood? There's one thing that doesn't seem to fit. I had understood that Andrew's father was . . . well, pretty hard on him. And that's what I saw on the bridge last night. But then last evening at the hospital—and again this morning—he seemed so gentle and so concerned about Andrew."

Alice sighed. "It's always been like that, Julie. My husband loves Andrew. Really, he does. He wants so much to be a good father to the boy. But . . . well, he doesn't seem to know *how* to be a good father. Sometimes he's so gentle and patient and kind. And then other times—most of the time, I guess—he just screams at Andrew, calls him names, drives him like a farm animal."

"Does he . . . I mean, has he ever . . . ?"

"Has he ever hit Andrew?"

Julie nodded.

"No, Julie. I've never known my husband to strike either his son or me. But I wonder sometimes if that would hurt any more than some of the things he says, and the way he says them.

"And he's obsessed with this 'work' thing—both for himself and for Andrew. It's as if no job is ever done well enough or soon enough. It's as though he needs to punish himself and his son for . . . for I don't know what. "Most of the time there seems to be a sort of false front or a mask, and that's when he's angry and abusive. And then other times—like when he's drunk, or when there's a real crisis—he lowers the mask and the *real* Jim Sherwood shows through."

"And the real Jim Sherwood is gentle and kind?"

"Very gentle. Very kind. Very warm. That's the Jim Sherwood I fell in love with. That's the Jim Sherwood I married."

Julie looked for a long time at the older woman. Then she said, "Mrs. Sherwood, I do hope you can get him back."

Sunday, January 31; morning [5 days to competition]

Alice Sherwood had finished feeding the chickens. As she stepped into the barn, her husband was just finishing the milking. Together they walked to the house, where Jim strained the milk and Alice washed the eggs and put them in the refrigerator.

"I'll get some breakfast started," Alice said.

"Good idea," replied her husband. "But keep it simple. We haven't much time."

"We haven't much time?"

"That's right, Mama. If we hurry, we can visit Andrew in the hospital and still get to Church on time."

Alice turned and stared at her husband.

Jim enjoyed her astonishment. "What's that look for, Girl?"

Still Alice said nothing.

"You want your boy back, don't you? Well, so do I. I reckon we need all the help we can get."

Alice smiled and blinked back tears of happiness. "Yes," she said. "We need all the help we can get."

The same day; evening

Jim and Alice Sherwood were sitting in Room 127, conversing quietly and holding hands. Jim took the watch from his pocket, looked at it, then returned it to his pocket.

"Almost time for dinner, Mama. You reckon maybe his appetite will wake him up pretty soon?"

"I hope so, Jim. He's been asleep for nearly two full days now."

"Doctor Feldman says it's all to the good. Says once he catches up on his rest, he'll probably be ready to get back into the harness."

"Yes, Papa. But . . . well, we've got to go easier on him."

"That's the truth, Mama. Dr. Feldman says a boy needs some time for work and some time to be a boy. Says he needs some time for school and some time to just be with other young folks."

"He's been so isolated . . . maybe we could get a telephone?"

"That's right! Money's better spent on a phone than on beer down at Coney Island!" There was a gentleness in Jim Sherwood's words.

"What else did you and the doctor talk about? I mean, you've been together most of yesterday and today."

"Lots of things. Mostly, we talked about how to raise boys."

"How to raise boys?"

"That's right. He told me some things that sure make good sense to me. Says you can always get more out of a boy with a pat on the back than with a kick in the butt."

"He said that?"

"Well, not in just those words, I reckon."

"What else, Papa? What else did he say?"

"Well, one thing he said hit me hard: he says a boy learns how to be a dad by watchin' his own dad."

"Do you suppose that's true?"

"Often enough, I reckon. Well, look at *me*: I hated Charlie. He yelled at me. He got drunk all the time. He beat up on my Ma and was cruel to me and my sister. With all my body and soul I hated that man! I swore I'd never be like him. But . . . ."

"But . . . ?"

"But darned if I don't talk and act and drink and rant and rave just like Charlie Catton did!"

"And you're afraid that Andrew . . . ?"

"I'm afraid so. He might turn out to be the same miserable excuse for a husband and father than I am—and that Charlie Catton was!"

There was a long pause as Alice tried to decide how to respond to that. Finally, she spoke. "So . . . what's to be done, Jim?"

"Simple. Dr. Feldman says someone's got to break the pattern. Sooner or later someone in one generation or another has to stop abusing his wife and kids. And it might just as well be *me*. "Maybe there's still time, Alice, to be a *real* husband to you—and a *real* father to this boy."

Alice Sherwood looked at her unconscious son and then at her husband and said very quietly, "That's all I've ever wanted, really."

A nurse entered the room and greeted Mr. and Mrs. Sherwood. As she started to check the patient's blood pressure and pulse, Andrew stirred, opened his eyes, and looked directly at his mother. Quickly, Jim knelt at the bedside and put a large, rough hand on his son's cheek.

"Son? It's your Pa. Are you hearin' me, Son?"

"Yes, Pa." Tears in his eyes, Jim turned to look at his wife, and saw her intense relief at this first evidence that Andrew's mind was going to be all right. The nurse left quickly to summon the doctors.

Suddenly, Andrew moved to get out of bed. "The cows! I've got to milk the cows."

Smiling, Jim Sherwood gently restrained the boy. "All done, Son. I did it myself, and Mama here, she took care of the chickens."

Alice kissed her son and patted his face. "I'm so glad to hear your voice, Son. We've been so afraid . . . ."

"Don't worry about nothin', Son. I'll take care of the chores for now. I reckon we can do 'em together . . . after you get to feelin' better, I mean. You and me—we both know how to work, don't we? Won't take hardly no time at all with us workin' together.

"And that dumb fence. Same thing: We'll do 'er together, and we will take our time doin' it, too."

Gently, Alice added, "And that will leave you some time to do the things you'd like to do."

Andrew's face clouded with concern as he recalled the band situation. He again moved to arise from his bed. "The band . . ." he said, then sank back onto his pillow.

"Son, Mr. Lesser said he would be here later tonight. You can talk with him about the band." Very gently, Jim Sherwood said, "As for me, Son well,

. . . I was all wrong tellin' you you couldn't be in the band. Will you forgive me, Son?"

Doctors Ahrens and Feldman appeared at the door. "Behold the resurrection of the dead!" said Dr. Ahrens. "We thought maybe you were going to sleep until school ends in June!"

Doctor Feldman turned to Andrew's parents. "I'll have to ask you folks to leave while we examine your son. But I can tell already that he's turned an important corner. I think we'll have good news for you."

12
Blossoms in Winter

The Same Night; later

As Mr. Lesser entered Room 127, the nurse was adjusting Andrew's I.V. The nurse left, and the band leader sat down.

"The doctors said I could visit with you for a minute, Mr. Sherwood. How are you feeling, Son?"

Very quietly, Andrew said, "I'm . . . I'm going to be fine, Sir."

"I . . . ah . . . I'm not sure how much you remember of what happened Friday."

"I remember missing the rehearsals before school and first period." The voice was flat, without emotion. "I remember . . . being cut from band for breaking training rules."

"I'm so very sorry about that. Andrew, I made a big mistake. At the very least I should have listened to you before making a decision . . . ."

"I'm afraid I let everybody down. I tried so hard to not let you down, Sir."

Mr. Lesser spoke very gently. "You didn't let us down, Andrew. If I had listened long enough to get the facts, I wouldn't have cut you from band." There was a long pause. "Will you forgive me? I'm asking you come back and be part of the band."

"But the training rules . . . . Everyone knows I missed a whole day's rehearsals. How can you . . . ?"

"Well, you're not alone, you know. I missed the Friday night rehearsal, too. We'll both have to throw ourselves on the mercy of the people in the band." There was a smile on Mr. Lesser's face.

"And you think . . . ?"

"I'm sure of it. I'll discuss it with everyone tomorrow morning. But I wouldn't worry about it, if I were you. By now everybody knows how hard you've worked to be there every time, on time. Everybody knows how you've skipped dinner night after night, how you've walked many miles home after rehearsals . . . and all the rest. Everybody knows you've worked harder at home and at school that anyone else in the band. I *know* they'll take *you* back." Again the band conductor smiled. "I'm not so sure they'll take *me* back!"

"Sir, you're saying that I'm in the band still?" He said it as though he hadn't supposed that such a thing was possible.

"Count on it."

"Well, if that don't beat all . . . ."

"*Doesn't*. If that *doesn't* beat all . . . ."

"Yes. That, too."

Mr. Lesser stood. "Now, I'd better leave you." Then he leaned down close to Andrew's ear and whispered, "By the way, one of the more decorative members of the band is waiting down the hall to visit you, if you're up to it . . . ."

"You mean . . . ?"

"Tall oboe player. Andrew? I sort of got the impression on the bridge that maybe she likes you."

"Yes, Sir. I believe she does. Thank you, Sir."

"Now, you get better as quickly as you can. If it's possible, we need to have you well enough to help us take State next Friday. Good night, Son. I can't tell you how glad I am that you are looking so much better."

Mr. Lesser left the room and walked down the hall, where he paused to speak with Julie. She rose from the sofa and asked, "Sir? Is he . . . ?"

"He's very much improved, Julie. And seeing *you* should make him even better! See you tomorrow morning in the band room."

Julie walked to the door of Room 127. In her hand she carried a white vase filled with fruit tree twigs—the same vase and the same twigs Andrew had delivered to her on Christmas Eve. Now each twig was covered with beautiful and fragrant blossoms, a perfume bouquet in pink and white.

Julie paused at the door before opening it, thinking about what this moment meant to the two of them. For nine weeks she and Andrew had been fond of each other, with a fondness which time had only strengthened—or at least she hoped Andrew was as fond of her as she thought he was. For nine weeks they had passed notes to each other in secret, rarely speaking aloud to one another. Now, for the first time ever, they were to be alone together and free to talk. She let out a quick breath and opened the door.

"Hi." Julie said somewhat shyly, but with a big smile. She put the vase and bouquet on Andrew's night stand.

"Hi."

"Mr. Lesser says you're feeling better."

"Yeah."

"Really?"

"Really. I'm fine."

Julie smiled. "I'm glad. You had us all worried on the bridge."

"I don't remember much about that."

"It was kinda scary. I . . . I was afraid you . . . ."

"Doc says I'm all right now. He says it probably will never happen again."

"I don't understand."

"Well, Pa says he's going to cut way back on my work at home. And Mr. Lesser says I still can be in the band. And, well, here *you* are, bringing me flowers, and . . . well, I'm feeling a lot better."

Julie smiled her warmest smile. "That's good. Well, come to think of it, you don't *sound* sick."

There was a pause. Andrew looked at Julie—right into her eyes—and then smiled without blushing very much.

"Is something funny?" she asked.

"No. No. I was just thinking. Well, I've been in the band with you for a long time, and sitting right next to you for three weeks now, and . . . ."

" . . . and we've never had a chance to talk?"

"Yes. I mean, just the two of us."

"I know. We've secretly passed notes to each other and all, but . . . it's not the same, is it?

"So many times I've thought about what I might say to you . . . if I ever got the chance. I mean, while I was walking home after rehearsals, I'd have long imaginary talks with you."

Julie was delighted. "And what did we talk about?"

"Oh, all kinds of things. School and friends and homework and band . . . you know, the kinds of things we'd say if we could go on dates or talk on the telephone."

"I know. I've had the same imaginary conversations. I feel as though I already know you well, Andrew."

"I . . . I'd like to . . . to know you better, Julie. You're . . . nice."

"There. I knew you'd say something just like that."

"You did?"

"Yes. Shy. But polite. Gentle. Soft-spoken. Sincere."

"Mostly shy, I guess. And scared to death of girls."

Julie smelled the apple blossoms in the bouquet on the night stand. "At first, these were just bare twigs, and look at them now!"

"Some kinds of flowers need a little more time before they blossom out . . . ."

" . . . or just to be brought in from the cold." Julie smiled and looked at Andrew again. Did he know that last comment had less to do with the flowers than with him?

"Julie? I think you're good for me. All my life I've looked in the mirror and figured no girl could ever like me. Now here you are telling me that you . . . ."

" . . . that I care for you; that I believe in you." She brightened. "And I'm not the only one. Look at this!" Julie produced a copy of Saturday's *Enterprise* from her coat pocket, and handed it to Andrew. "Front page."

Andrew read aloud as he scanned the story. "' . . . baritone sax player . . . learning the bassoon part at the last minute . . . walking seven miles home in the rain after rehearsals every night . . . digging stumps by hand . . . farm chores . . . Clark Kent in the woodwind section.' Julie? This is just . . . well . . . it's . . . ."

"I told you my Daddy liked you."

"Clark Kent?"

"I suggested that part, because you have big arms and shoulders . . . ."

"But Clark Kent?"

"Anyway, now everyone in town knows what I've known for a long time—that you're a very special person."

Andrew said it once more, in an incredulous whisper: "Clark Kent?"

"Now, I'd better leave. You're repeating yourself, and about to have a relapse. Besides, Dr. Feldman said I couldn't stay too long."

Andrew brightened. "I'm so glad you came. You . . . you're the best medicine of all for me."

Julie leaned down and planted a small kiss directly in the center of Andrew's forehead. "Goodnight, Andrew. I'll see you again tomorrow after school."

As Julie pulled away, she looked at Andrew. His eyes were closed and he said nothing, but his face and neck were turning bright red. She smiled and took his hand in hers, saying nothing for about a minute.

"Julie?" he finally said, his eyes still closed, "the competition is . . . is only five days away and I haven't even *looked* at Shostakovich for . . . for three days now. And who knows when they'll let me out of here. Do you think you could . . . maybe could smuggle my sax into here?"

Julie frowned. "Is that wise? You're supposed to be resting."

"Clark Kent resting?" Andrew's eyes flipped open wide. "With Metropolis in danger?"

Julie laughed. "I'd need some help . . . ."

"Call Chuck and Wally. They'd be happy to help with something that sounds illegal."

"Perfect! We'll be back within the hour." From the doorway Julie blew one more small kiss at Andrew and said, "Goodnight."

As the door shut softly behind her, Andrew's look of amazement slowly melted into an awkward smile. "Goodnight," he said to the closed door.

Monday, February 1; before school [4 days to competition]

"People," Mr. Lesser began, "I know each one of you understands why I wasn't here for Friday night's rehearsal. And I'm sure you've all heard by now that Mr. Sherwood is much improved. I'm told that he even has a bassoon disguised as a baritone sax in his hospital room. And I think there is little doubt that Mr. Sherwood will be with us for the competition next Friday. As to the training rules—well, he really does have 'a note from the hospital.'

"We've had strict training rules, People—maybe too strict. Where I have held *you* so strictly to those rules, I think it only fair that you have an opportunity to hold *me* to the same rules. I hereby kick myself out of concert band—for missing Friday night's rehearsal.

"With myself out of the band, I appoint Mr. Swinton director-pro-tem."

Barry Swinton acted swiftly. "I move that Mr. Lesser be reinstated immediately."

"Second the motion," said Carole Larsen.

"Further move that the vote be by acclamation."

"Second the motion," said Carole again.

"All those in favor say 'aye.'"

"Aye."

Barry finished the little charade. "The chair rules that Mr. Lesser is reinstated by acclamation."

"Mr. Chairman?" said Wally Arnold.

"The chair recognizes the pizzaholic in the percussion section."

"Mr. Chairman, we really could use one more pair of hands in the percussion section, especially in the last two minutes of the Finale. I move that Arlene Simmons also be reinstated to turn pages for the percussion section."

Before Carole could second the motion, Mr. Lesser interrupted. "May I?"

Carole nodded.

"I second the motion that Miss Simmons be reinstated and assigned to the percussion section."

"All in favor say 'aye.'" "Aye!"

Arlene Simmons—the *new* Arlene Simmons—was back in Concert Band.

"May I add something?" asked Mr. Lesser. "For years, music was the only thing in my life. I dreamed of conducting a great orchestra in one of the great cities. But the reality is that there are a lot more would-be conductors than there are great orchestras—and in the meantime you've got to buy groceries and pay the rent.

"For a while I taught in Ashland. Then I came to Oregon City High. I guess I resented having to listen to high-school band music, when what I really wanted was the New York Philharmonic. I guess I began to act out my own little Philharmonic fantasy when I challenged each of you to pay the price and take State. Taking State became the most important thing in my life, and woe to anything or anybody who got in my way.

"Well, in the last few weeks—and especially this weekend—I've come to realize that there is something more important than taking State or conducting a great orchestra. What a high school band teacher does is teach kids the important lessons of life. I guess nothing could be more important or satisfying than teaching kids about decency and self-control and goal-setting. But I've also learned that even good things can be carried too far, that along with justice there must be mercy, and that *people* are more important than trophies and applause.

"Win, lose, or draw, kids, I love each one of you, and I thank God for you."

Same Day; mid-morning

Doctor Feldman approached the nurses' station where two nurses were seated. "Music?" he asked. "What music? Do you ladies hear music?"

One nurse turned to the other and said, "I don't hear music. I certainly don't hear a baritone sax, do you?"

"Not me," replied the other nurse. "Nor an oboe, for that matter."

Doctor Feldman smiled. "Well, even though none of us can hear music, it might be well to move Mr. Sherwood to a room at the far end of the hall, as far as possible from those poor patients who seem to be hearing things, like baritone saxes and oboes."

Tuesday, February 2; evening *[3 days to competition]*

Andrew, dressed in the new flannel pajamas his mother had made for him, was sitting on his hospital bed, talking with his parents while doing homework. "So, when are they going to let me out of here?" he asked.

"Soon, Son. Soon, I'm sure."

"That's right. They'll release you when they're sure you're ready."

"When I'm *ready?* I'm doing homework. I'm practicing my baritone. I'm eating everything in sight. What do I have to do to prove I'm ready to go home?"

Andrew's father laughed. "All in good time, Boy. All in good time."

Alice Sherwood looked at the clock. "It's getting late, Papa. We'd better leave so Andrew can get some sleep." Then she turned to Andrew and smiled. "Besides, Papa promised to take me to Chicken-in-a-Basket on the way home!"

Very quietly, very happily, Andrew said, "Ah, that's nice. That's real nice."

She continued. "Son, I think something good is going to come out of all of this. We—your Pa and I—we haven't been this close in years."

Jim Sherwood nodded in agreement. "And Doctor Feldman has been helping me learn some important things about myself—why I've acted the way I have—and how to be a better father, too. Reckon I needed something like this to wake me up, Son, to make me realize how much I love your Ma and how proud I am of my boy. I've even come to where I can speak kindly of my poor old step-dad, Charlie.

"Good night, Son." The soft-spoken, kindly—stone sober—Jim Sherwood kissed his son on the cheek and told him how much he loved him.

Andrew's tear ducts chose this particular moment to make both seeing and speaking harder than usual. "I . . . I love you, too, Pa. You . . . You go on now, and take this pretty girl out for dinner, like you promised her."

As Andrew's parents left, a nurse appeared and asked Andrew, "Are you up to one more visit tonight? There are some young people here from the band."

"Do they have anything with them to eat?"

"They'd better *not* have!" The nurse turned to the group in the hall and opened the door. "All right, you guys. Five minutes, no more. And no music. And keep the noise down."

Chuck laughed, "All right, Sarge, we'll be good boys and girls."

Entering the room, Wally asked Andrew, "Now, what is going *on* here?"

"Yeah, Sweetie," said Chuck. "Where were *you* during tonight's rehearsal?"

Barry supplied the answer. "Where was *he*? He was laying on his butt in *bed!*"

"Yeah! Being spoon fed!" This time it was Darryl.

"And with some cute little nurse holding his hand," guessed Chuck.

"Holding his hand?" Julie had some serious reservations.

"Oh, oh! *Now* you're in trouble, Sherwood!" said Wally in mock seri-ousness.

"Any hand-holding here will be done by *Julie!*" said Carole.

"That's right. You're all done flirting with nurses, Son," said Darryl. "Your local authorized oboe dealer has put her license plate on your back bumper!"

Julie called the group to order. "Enough, already! Do you want that drill-sergeant back in here?"

Wally winked at Andrew. "See? They're all like that. *All* females are bossy. It's because most females are girls."

This was something Andrew had been missing most of his life: friends to talk with and laugh with. "Hey . . . it . . . it is really great to see you guys. Thanks for coming."

Chuck tried finishing Andrew's sentence for him, " . . . and now why don't you dummies get out of here so I can be alone with Julie!"

"No . . . no. Seriously, I . . . I've always wanted to just be one of the guys."

The mood suddenly turned serious as they were reminded of how little they had tried to be Andrew's friend until now. "Hey, you had us worried for a while, Babe," Chuck said. "That was bad news on the bridge last Friday night."

"Are you sure you're going to be all right?" Barry asked.

Embarrassed by all the attention, Andrew looked down. Julie squeezed his hand and said, "Andrew is going to be fine."

"Listen, Sherwood, we . . . none of us had any idea what you were going through. Why didn't you tell somebody you needed a ride home after rehearsals?"

"I . . . I didn't want to bother anybody and I didn't . . . I didn't think anybody would . . . . I mean, nobody lives that far out Redland Road."

"Hey, Sweetums, what are friends *for?* When you got a problem, you tell your friends, don't you?"

"I . . . I didn't think you . . . you guys . . . ."

Darryl spoke to Wally: "For a smart guy, he's kinda dumb, you know?" Then he turned to Andrew. "Sherwood, you're not alone. You got *friends.*"

"Yeah, Sweetie." Chuck looked around to make sure no drill sergeants were watching. "And here's proof positive. What do friends bring their friends in prison?" Andrew looked puzzled. "They bring them *food!*" From inside his coat, Chuck produced a hamburger, fries, and a bottle of Orange Crush.

Wally added, "And what else do friends bring their friends in the slammer? They bring beautiful *weemin'!*" Wally said the last word with great exaggeration, pointing at Julie.

The nurse appeared at the door, and Andrew quickly hid the contraband calories.

"Oh, oh! Too loud, right, Sarge?" Wally showed a notable lack of contrition.

"Right! Out with you, *all* of you. This poor, sick child needs his rest."

Barry picked up on that comment. "Poor sick child? Right! Sarge, what this poor sick child needs is for someone to swat his poor sick butt!"

And Chuck: "It looks like a good life to me: no school, no rehearsals . . . ."

"Listen, Sherwood, you can't fool *us.* You're not sick, so knock it off with the faking. We need you for the competition Friday."

"That's right. As sure as God made little green apples sour, Oregon City is going to take State three days from now!"

Very quietly Andrew vowed, "I'll be there. Whatever else may happen, I *will* be there."

After his friends had left, Andrew ate the very first hamburger and fries of his life.

Wednesday, February 3; morning [2 days to competition]

Mr. Wallace Arnold sat at his very large executive's desk, dialing his telephone. On the highly polished desk was a copy of last Saturday's *Enterprise*.

"Hello? Mr. Cochran? Wally here. Yes, Wallace Arnold at Crown-Zellerbach. Listen, I've been reading this piece in the paper about the Sherwood boy and hearing a lot about him from my own son. Yes . . . . Yes . . . . But I'm told he's doing much better now . . . . That's good . . . . Fine . . . glad to hear it . . . . And you think he'll be there Friday for the state band competition? . . . .

"Well, I've got a hot flash I'd like to run past you. Wally says the boy is bright enough, and a hard worker, but his folks may not be in a position to send him to college next Fall . . . . Yes . . . I see . . . That's about what I had gathered.

"You know, after we paid for the new band uniforms, we had quite a bit of money left over, and we weren't quite sure how best to use it. What would you think if we used it as a scholarship for the Sherwood boy? Yes . . . I think so, too . . . .

"Well, as principal you're in a better position to work out those kinds of details . . . . Yes, Mr. Cochran. I'm glad you agree . . . ."

13
The Picnic

The same day; mid-day

As Doctor Ahrens entered Andrew's room, he found the boy dressed in pajamas and practicing his baritone sax.

"On your feet, Sherwood," said the doctor with a smile. "We're kicking you out of here."

"You mean I can leave? Now?"

"Well, I guess you'd *better* leave. We only allow sick people to stay, and you aren't sick. Plus, your music is a menace to people who really are sick. And anyway, the hospital is going broke trying to feed you!"

"I was going to ask about that," Andrew started. "How come I didn't get lunch today? I'm starving!"

"We didn't feed you because we got a call from someone who asked us *not* to feed you. She's waiting for you in the lobby with a picnic lunch."

"A picnic lunch? That's . . . that's great! Just give me a second to get dressed, Doctor, and I'll be gone!" A nurse arrived with a wheelchair, and was surprised that Andrew put the saxophone case in the wheelchair and began pushing it toward the elevator.

"Wait! *You're* supposed to ride in the wheelchair . . . ."

"The Doctor says I'm not sick. It's this poor saxophone that needs . . . that needs some rest!" Andrew turned to the nurse. "Thanks, Sarge, I appreciate . . . I mean you really are one of the good guys. And Doctor Ahrens? Thanks. Thank you very much for . . . for helping me. Now, if you'll excuse me, I think it's lunch time."

"Do you think it's the picnic lunch that has him in such a rush?" asked the nurse.

"More likely the girl," observed Doctor Ahrens dryly.

Andrew grinned sheepishly as all three entered the elevator and started down one floor to the lobby.

Julie stepped toward Andrew as the elevator door opened, a happy smile on her face. "Are you all right?" she asked. "Can you leave now?"

"Can I *leave?* Julie, I think . . . I think they're throwing me out of here. And without . . . without having fed me!"

Dr. Feldman had joined the little group. "Julie, we'll turn him over to you. Go feed him! Get him out of here! We have work to do. His father took care of all the paperwork this morning."

Andrew and Julie took the baritone sax case and left, waving thanks as they went. Julie opened the trunk of her father's car so Andrew could put the heavy instrument case inside. There Andrew saw the picnic basket Doctor Ahrens had mentioned.

"Doc says you brought a rescue kit . . . and I'm about ready for it! I haven't had a thing to eat for a couple of hours!"

"Not so fast. You can't eat a picnic lunch standing in a hospital parking lot."

Julie started the car. "Where to?" she asked.

"A picnic spot? You know, I haven't been on a whole lot of picnics. Come to think of it, I don't think I've *ever* been on a picnic."

"Say, this is a great date. *I* fix the lunch. *I* line up the car. *I* come to your house and pick you up. *I* drive the car. And now *I* have to decide where we're going?"

"Aren't we going to school? Isn't this a school day? Don't we have a lunch-time rehearsal?"

"No. Yes. No. Any other questions?"

"What?"

"No, we're *not* going to school, because your doctors said for you to take it easy. Yes, this is a school day. And no, we don't have a rehearsal. It's too late. And we have all afternoon before the after-school rehearsal."

"What about our classes?"

"Would you rather spend the afternoon with Mr. Goodmanson or with me?"

"Would Mr. Goodmanson feed me?"

"I doubt it."

"Then, I choose you."

There was a pause as Julie looked Andrew straight in the eyes. "And I choose you."

Julie found a secluded picnic area in a woodsy creek-side setting. It being a weekday afternoon in February, there were no other picnickers around. The weather was clear and unseasonably warm, but both of them were glad they had dressed warmly.

As Julie cleared away the wreckage of what had been a nice picnic lunch, Andrew said, "That was wonderful! I'm glad I chose *you* instead of Mr. Goodmanson."

"And I'm glad I chose *you*."

Andrew's voice and countenance turned serious. "That's . . . that's something I've wondered about. Why *me*, Julie? Why not somebody else?"

"Hmmm?"

"There are so many other guys and . . . I'm . . . ."

"You were tall."

"Tall?"

Julie opened a box of crackerjacks and poured its contents onto a paper plate. Then she spoke as though she were a math teacher presenting a story problem to her class. "A certain girl attends a small high school of 492 students. Half the students are girls." Julie separated the crackerjacks into two piles. "This leaves how many potential boys for the girl to date?"

"About two-hundred-fifty . . . ?"

"Good, Class! Now, one-fourth of these are freshmen and the girl in question will *not* date freshmen!" Julie moved one-fourth of the remaining crackerjacks to the first pile. "What do we have left?"

"Maybe one-hundred-eighty fellows."

"One-hundred-seventy-six, to be precise. Now this certain girl—a lovely, talented young thing, you understand—happens to be somewhat tall. She's five-foot-twelve, as a matter of fact. If we assume that she's not likely to be asked out by fellows who are shorter than she is, how many boys are left?"

"Two, three dozen?"

Julie moved all the remaining crackerjacks except eleven to the larger pile. "Exactly eleven boys."

"Eleven?"

"Eleven. But two are freshmen." Each time she spoke, Julie moved more of the remaining crackerjacks to the larger pile.

"Nine left."

And one of the nine is engaged to be married."

"Eight."

"And one has been at Fort Benning for two months now."

"Seven to go."

"And three others are going steady."

"Four left."

"But three of the remaining four are absolute creeps. The charming and vivacious young lady of whom we speak—a stunning, brown-eyed brunette—may be tall, but she is not desperate."

"One left."

Julie picked up the one remaining crackerjack and considered it closely. "The tall saxophone player with the gentle blue eyes and the Clark Kent physique gets an 'A' in math!"

"So . . . because I'm six-foot-three, you . . . ?"

"Yes. At first." Julie could see the hurt in Andrew's eyes. "At first that's all I saw. But then I began to learn some other things about you—things that are a lot more important than just height. I learned that you are gentle and kind, and that you work hard after everyone else has quit. I learned that you control your temper and your language. I learned that those who know you best have nothing but praise for you."

"Did you also learn that I can't call you up? Or get to the Saturday dances? Or drive over to see you? Your math problem ends with a tall, very pretty girl looking for a date and getting no dates at all."

"What if she got to sit right next to the boy several hours a day in band rehearsals? And isn't she on a date right now?"

"But nine weeks' work to . . . to line up one picnic?"

"The girl of whom we speak is persistent. And maybe she'd prefer an occasional picnic with the right boy to going steady with somebody else. Maybe the girl in the story problem thinks she's found a real crackerjack."

Andrew reached into the pile of crackerjacks and removed the toy prize. He considered it carefully, then said to Julie, "You . . . you may or may not have a crackerjack. But I'm the one who got the prize!"

After they had put the picnic basket in the trunk of the car, Julie and Andrew took a walk along the creek-side path, talking, laughing, and throwing crackerjacks to the ducks.

In a sunlit flowerbed in the shelter of a huge red cedar tree, they discovered crocuses and trilliums, the year's earliest flowers—blossoms in winter.

"Funny, I've always been so shy and afraid. I've never had a girlfriend or even a date. But now with you I don't feel shy or afraid."

Julie took Andrew's hand, and saw that he didn't flinch or blush. "Do you realize that until Sunday evening we had never even had a real talk?"

"Or been alone together."

"And here we are, talking, feeding the ducks, even holding hands."

"And ditching school. I think you're corrupting me."

"You'd rather be with Mr. Goodmanson?"

"Are you *sure* he wouldn't feed me?"

"Andrew, the man dissects frogs!"

Andrew turned to face Julie, and took both her hands in his. "I'd choose you. Julie, I'd choose you even if you didn't feed me." Julie smiled and moved closer.

"I'm so glad you . . . I mean . . . Julie, I'm so proud that you're my . . . ." Andrew couldn't quite speak the most important word in the sentence.

" . . . that I'm your girl?"

Andrew looked away. "Is . . . Is that what you are?"

"I hope so."

Andrew looked into her eyes. "I hope so, too."

The mood was becoming uncomfortably serious for either of them, so they resumed their stroll. Smiling, Andrew said, "Julie, I can't quite believe that all of this is happening to me. I never thought a girl—*any* girl—let alone someone pretty like you—could want to be *my* girl, or go on a picnic with me, or hold my hand, or . . . ."

Julie turned to Andrew and teased him with a flirting smile. " . . . or kiss you?"

Andrew was back to blushing—the USDA Number One variety. "Say, didn't your mother . . . didn't your mother teach you that girls . . . that girls are supposed to be coy?"

Julie smiled impishly. "No. My father taught me to decide what I want and to go after it. Short girls can be coy. Article Nine of the Geneva Convention on Love and War says the tallest girl in any high school can make up her own rules."

"But I've never . . . I mean . . . I don't think I know how to . . . ."

Now it was Julie who turned her eyes away. "I've never kissed anyone either."

Gently, only their hands touching, Andrew and Julie drew still closer to each other, and shared love's first brief, tender, awkward kiss. They opened their eyes, their faces still very close, and looked at each other for several seconds, neither quite believing what had just happened.

Julie spoke first: "Merry Christmas."

"Uh . . . . It's February."

"I didn't give you a present at Christmas."

Andrew laughed. "It was worth waiting for."

They continued walking, saying nothing for a time. They found a redwood bench at the side of a pond where they could sit.

"Andrew? In the hospital you told me about the imaginary conversations we had while you walked home in the dark. Did we . . . did we ever talk about the future?"

"Lots of times."

"Like what?" Julie asked eagerly.

"Well, careers, and how large a family we'd like to have, and . . . ."

Delighted, Julie laughed. "We're on our very first date, and already we're deciding how many children we're going to have?"

Andrew was completely flustered. "I didn't mean . . . I mean . . . I meant . . . well . . . how many each of us might . . . ."

Julie sat closer and squeezed Andrew's hand. "It's all right, Goose. I didn't mean to embarrass you. I know what you meant. It's like I told you, I've had the same imaginary conversations. Except in mine we actually *did* talk about the family we'll have some day."

There was a very long pause as Andrew sorted out the implications of Julie's last statement. "And what did we decide?"

"We decided to have three tall boys and two tall girls—after you go to college, where you'll become a famous scientist and win the Nobel Prize and be elected president and . . . ."

Andrew was incredulous. "Whoa! I'm going to college? And becoming a scientist?"

" . . . or something. Of course you are. You have a fine mind and so many talents, you can be anything you want to be . . . ."

" . . . if you're willing to pay the price. I know. I've heard that ten thousand times in the band room. But, Julie, I'm . . . I'm just a farm boy from a poor family. Nobody in my family ever . . . ever went to college. And besides, I'm ugly and dumb and . . . ."

"Ugly and dumb?" There was fire in Julie's flashing eyes. "You are *not* ugly! You are *not* dumb! And if your father told you so ten-thousand times, it still wouldn't be so! You're very handsome, and every girl in school knows it, even if you don't! And what's so dumb about straight "A's"?

"And I suppose I'm not shy and awkward either."

"A young racehorse starts out awkward, too. Andrew, you've got to have confidence in yourself. You are not awkward. If you're shy, you'll overcome it. You can be *anything* you want to be!"

"How can you be so sure?"

"My Daddy told me so. He's been telling me that ever since I was a little girl."

"So. I'm going to go to college and become a great . . . ."

" . . . a great something. You decide what."

"And you're going to become . . . ?"

"I'm going to become the wife of a great somebody, and a great writer who wins a Pulitzer Prize. And you'd better watch out, Andrew Sherwood, or we might wind up with the same last name!"

Amazed, Andrew looked at the girl and smiled at her intensity. "Sounds like . . . like premeditated matrimony!"

Julie laughed out loud—a laugh of pure delight. "In the first degree! Guilty as charged, Your Honor."

Again Andrew paused as he always did before expressing his most serious thoughts. "Julie? I like you lot, and you like me, and that makes me the happiest guy in Clackamas County. But . . . well, we're both just seventeen and we're both new at this dating business, and . . ."

"I know. We have to go slowly. I agree. We need to have lots of time to get to know each other—lot of dates and double dates. Probably, we each should date other people, too. My Daddy has told me all of that, and I agree. But for now, I'm your girl, and you're my fellow. All right?"

"All right and then some. Julie . . ." he strained against his own embarrassment. "I think I like you very much."

"I've waited a long time to hear you say that, Andrew."

"If I said it often, would that make up for the wait?"

"It would help."

Andrew looked down and paused again. He nervously tried to cover an embarrassed smile.

"What is it?" Julie asked. "What are you thinking about?"

He smiled an awkward smile and turned and faced her. "What about New Years'?" he asked.

"New Years'?"

"You didn't give me a New Years' present either."

Julie smiled, then leaned over and kissed Andrew again. It was a gentle kiss, as before, but slightly longer and less awkward.

This time Andrew didn't look away as they finished. "I . . . I guess we'd better leave, hadn't we?" he said. "Dmitri Shostakovich is waiting for us in the band room." Arm in arm, hand in hand, Andrew and Julie strolled back to the car.

14
The Finale

Thursday, February 4; evening [1 day to competition]

Usually, when Oregon City High School staged a pep rally and bonfire, it was a fairly anemic affair. It is difficult to generate much excitement when everyone knows that the home team is going to lose.

Tonight, things were different. The members of the band *knew* they were ready. They took great pride in their beautiful, brand-new red and white uniforms. Beyond that, everyone else in town knew what the band members knew: Oregon City had a good shot at taking State.

On this, the night before the State Band Competition, a monster pep rally and bonfire were in progress at Kelly Field. Not only were band members present, but the whole student body—and their teachers and their parents, and just about anyone in town with a link to the high school.

The fire department was there, too, as if a February bonfire in Oregon somehow could burn anything without a lot of coaxing. Also present was the town's small police force—in case anyone from West Linn High got a notion to crash the party or remind Oregon City of its permanent "loser" status.

After the enormous bonfire had died down somewhat, Mr. Lesser stepped to the temporary platform and addressed the large crowd.

"We—the band members and I—are pleased that so many of you showed up for this rally. Some of the earlier rallies this year could have been held in a clothes closet." The crowd laughed.

"We've been working really hard now for ten weeks, getting ready for tomorrow's competition. And we think we're ready!"

Mr. Lesser was interrupted by a spontaneous cheer from the crowd.

"We think we're ready to go to Portland tomorrow and take State!"

An even larger cheer arose from the crowd, then "Take State! Take State! Take State!"

Mr. Lesser waited for the chant to die down. "Every one of these band members—and I mean every one of them—has worked really hard to get ready. They've rehearsed before school and again at first period. They've rehearsed during their lunch hours. They've been in the band room working after school and then again in the evening for sectional and full-band rehearsals. They've practiced endless hours at home. Let's have a nice round of applause for the members of the finest concert band in the State of Oregon!"

Applause. Loud whistles. Cheering.

"Section leaders: Come up here on the platform. I'd like another cheer for these section leaders, who not only have perfected their own execution, but have worked with others to get them ready, too."

Another cheer.

"And could I single out one player for special praise? Mr. Sherwood, come on up here." Andrew Sherwood, shy-for-life but growing in confidence, took his place in the limelight.

"Julie! Julie!" the other band members began chanting. "Julie! Julie!" A tall, very pretty oboe player emerged from the crowd to stand at Andrew's side, holding his hand. Andrew was cheered heartily when, in full view of the whole world, he put one arm around Julie's waist. The members of the band whistled and cheered as if Andrew had just intercepted a West Linn pass and returned it ninety-six yards for the winning touchdown.

Mr. Lesser waited again for the noise to die down before continuing. "This young man has done double duty, or triple. While carrying a huge work load on the family farm, and while maintaining top grades, he first learned the tenor sax part to perfection, then had to step in near the end and learn another very difficult, very important part. Could I have a cheer for Andrew Sherwood, alias Clark Kent?" Everyone in the audience had read the story, and responded with laughter and applause.

"Andrew?" Mr. Lesser asked, "Is there something you'd like to say to all these folks?"

A boy who previously could not speak to even one human being without stammering now faced a large crowd. Frightened still, but blossoming rapidly, Andrew Sherwood managed to say, "We . . . we're ready. We're going to . . . to take State!" Again the crowd responded with a cheer you could hear all the way to West Linn.

Then the cheerleaders took their turn, and discovered that cheerleading can be fun when the crowd thinks their team might actually win something. As always, Coach Ellis was called up to lead the crowd's favorite cheer—the cheer he had invented:

> "City Water
> City Gas
> We got West Linn
> By the . . . ankle!"

There were other speakers. Mr. Cochran spoke of bands and character and belonging and discovering what one is capable of. Mr. Arnold represented the city's service organizations as he told of how the band's new uniforms had come to be.

Barry Swinton called for a cheer for Mr. Lesser. "This is the man who has made it happen. This is the man who's been in the band room every day and every night. If we take State—*when* we take State—it will be because this man made it happen. The New York Philharmonic should be so lucky!"

It was true. Every person at Kelly Field knew it was true, and their cheers showed that they knew.

But it was Alton Ryckman who got the biggest cheer of the night—when he held up a preview copy of next Saturday's *Oregon City Enterprise*. The entire front page was filled with a headline: *PIONEER BAND TAKES STATE!*

Friday, February 5; morning [Competition Day]

As the members of the band rode to Portland on the school bus, there was none of the previous evening's brave talk. Most of the students had their own thoughts, their own concerns. Each student knew that however good he might be, he still fell short of "perfection"—if that truly was the required standard. Most hoped to do their best—and above all, to avoid being the person who might cause the judges to mark a demerit on Oregon City's score sheet.

The bus pulled into the bus-filled parking lot at Thomas Jefferson High School in Portland. To the side of one large bus was taped a paper banner reading "Ontario Take State." To another was taped "Astoria Take State." And so on through Medford and Hood River and Salem and Eugene and Coos Bay and Tigard and Baker and a great many more. No banners decorated Oregon City's bus: Mr. Lesser had suggested that the Pioneers save their boasting for later—*after* the competition.

The driver turned off the motor, and Mr. Lesser stood at the front of the bus. "People," he began, "we'll have a room inside the school where we store our things and where we can talk while we wait our turn to compete. But let me say before we even get off the bus that I expect you not only to *play* like the best band in the state today, but to *behave* like the best band. I will tolerate no boasting, no bragging. There will be no taunting of others, no booing. If someone does something well, applaud them. If someone does something poorly, say nothing.

"When we leave here, I want every person at this competition to go home saying that Oregon City's band played the best and looked the best and acted the best in the state. I know I can count on each one of you."

Entering the large high school, the band members saw the four registration tables, one for each of the various sizes of high schools in the state. Proudly, they walked past the 1-A registration table, where the West Linn band conductor was filling out the registration papers for his band.

"Morning, Ervin," said Mr. Thurgood of West Linn.

"Morning, John," nodded Mr. Lesser.

"Not as many of us in the 1-A competition as we've had some other years," observed Mr. Thurgood.

"Is that so? I'm sorry to hear that," said Oregon City's conductor. "Maybe some of the 1-A bands are competing in the higher divisions— competing with the larger schools." Then he excused himself and got in the 4-A line to register.

"Oregon City?" asked the registrar with astonishment. "Oregon City wants to compete in 4-A? We've never had a 1-A school compete at the 4-A level before."

"I believe the rules permit us to compete at any level. Isn't that right?" asked Mr. Lesser, knowing full well what the rules permitted.

"Oh, yes, certainly. Smaller schools can always compete at higher levels. It's right here in the rule book. But are you sure you . . . ?"

"We're sure. Now may I register, please?"

"Of course. But, Mr . . . ? Lesser, is it? You are new to band competition at the high school level, I believe. We have a tradition of excellence among our 4-A schools in this state, and I'd hate to see your students embarrassed simply because their conductor was new and registered them in the wrong level of competition. Are you quite sure you . . . ?"

"We'll try not to be an embarrassment to you or to ourselves. Now where do I register?"

"If you'll just fill out this form . . . . But this *does* present a bit of a problem, Mr. Lesser. You see, we always have the 4-A competition in the evening hours, and we of course assumed that Oregon City would be competing in 1-A, and we . . . . Well, we have already announced performance times for the 4-A competition, and . . . ."

"What's the problem?" asked Mr. Lesser.

"Well, it's too late to juggle the schedule now, I guess. I mean, it's already been printed in the newspapers. As a 1-A school, and newcomers to the 4-A competition, you really ought to compete first, but I suppose we'll just have to have you compete last."

"And you were hoping that Jefferson High could compete last?" asked Mr. Lesser, a knowing smile on his face. "You were hoping to save the best time slot for the perennial winner of the competition? Well, as I said before, we'll try to not embarrass you."

The band members left their instruments and coats in the locked room assigned to Oregon City High School, then went to the huge auditorium where the competition already was under way.

A small band from Myrtle Creek was working its way through "Egmont" Overture by Beethoven. To these band members who had paid the full price to achieve excellence, it was apparent that the little band from Douglas County had not. And it was apparent that the judges at the scoring table in the middle of the auditorium were finding plenty of demerits to note on their score sheets.

At the conclusion of "Egmont," the four judges tallied their scores and averaged them to obtain a competition score. Next to the name "Myrtle Creek" on the huge tally board to the left of the stage was put "Fair—69."

Sixty-nine. Fair. It was understood that no school ever was given a score lower than 60, and that "fair" was the lowest description awarded. What sixty-nine and "fair" really meant was "pretty awful."

The 1-A band from Reedsport was next. First their conductor distributed music scores to each of the four judges, who shook her hand and wished her well. Then she took her place in front of her band and led them in a good rendition of the "Washington Post" march. Again, the judges made their marks. Again, the average of the combined scores was posted. Next to the name "Reedsport" was posted "82—very good."

Eighty-two. Very good. That was about where Oregon City usually scored when competing with other small schools. How would they score today against the biggest high schools and the finest bands in the state?

Next on stage was the band from little Hermiston High School in Umatilla County. The judges received their copies of Stravinsky's "Firebird Suite" score, and wished the conductor well. The elderly band teacher stepped to the podium, brought down his baton, and the music began.

Each judge began with a blank sheet of paper before him. Each time he heard a mistake, he noted one demerit on the paper. It was all very simple. A band started with 100 points, and ended with 100 if none of the judges heard any mistakes. The easier the competition piece selected, the more strict the judges tended to be in their grading.

Hermiston finished their performance. The audience—mostly students from other high schools awaiting their turns to perform—rewarded Hermiston with warm applause. The judges tallied their scores and updated the tally board. Hermiston scored 92—excellent.

So it continued throughout the morning. West Linn scored 89—"Very Good," and the Oregon City band members applauded politely. Lakeview was awarded a 70—"Good." Hood River pulled out a 94—"Excellent."

When all the 1-A bands had competed, little Ashland High School— with so many of Mr. Lesser's former students—was crowned State 1-A Champions. With 96 points and a "Superior" for Smetena's incredible "Overture to the Bartered Bride," they were the best of Oregon's small school bands.

When the Oregon City band members returned from the cafeteria, they discovered that during the lunch break someone had scrawled "Losers" next to "Oregon City" on the tally board. Certain that they knew the source of this indignity, Wally and Chuck were ready to have it out with the entire West Linn band, but were cut short by Mr. Lesser.

"Remember what I told you on the bus," he said sternly. "I want not one word—not even one dirty look from any of you for West Linn or anyone else. We'll let our performance talk for us." Eventually, one of the competition officials taped a blank piece of paper over the word "losers," but not until everyone at the competition had seen it.

The 2-A competition continued. Klamath Falls took an 88 for a rating of "Very Good." Bend and Grants Pass both scored 78—"Good." Roseburg

High School did a good job on the very difficult "First Romanian Rhapsody" and won the 2-A Competition with a 94—"Excellent."

The State 3-A Competition continued through the late afternoon. McMinnville scored an embarrassing 65—"Fair." Beaverton took a 90—"Excellent." Several schools were clustered in the 80's—"Very Good." As usual, it was Milwaukee High School which won the 3-A Competition, scoring a 96—"Superior" for their brilliant performance of Bach's "Tocata and Fugue."

After dinner the schedule called for performances by six schools in the State 4-A Competition. The tally board showed the order of performance:

> Woodrow Wilson H.S.
> Eugene Central H.S.
> Abraham Lincoln H.S.
> George Washington H.S.
> Thomas Jefferson H.S.
> Oregon City H.S.

With the competition taking place on a Friday night, and with all of the six schools being either from Portland or reasonably close to Portland, it was not surprising that the huge auditorium was filled to capacity and overflowing. Where earlier in the day the audience had been made up of band members, conductors and bus drivers, it now also included parents, teachers, newspaper reporters—even a crew from a local television station.

First up was Wilson High. A very large band from a very large high school, Woodrow Wilson performed a vigorous and well-rehearsed rendition of Rossini's "An Italian Girl in Algeria" and earned an enthusiastic response from the huge audience. The judges awarded Woodrow Wilson a score of 95, just one point short of "superior."

Then Eugene Central High School took their places on stage as their conductor consulted with the judges. He gave the officials their copies of Beethoven's "Eroica," and shook their hands. Striding to the podium, he spoke quietly to his band, then lifted his baton.

"Eroica" is a marvelous piece of music, and well suited to impressing judges. But Eugene Central hadn't paid the price, and the audience could tell it. Worse, the judges could tell it. Next to "Eugene Central H.S." on the tally board was recorded 80—"Very Good."—just *barely* "very good"— only one point better than "good."

Abraham Lincoln High School did considerably better, earning a 93—
"Excellent" for their performance of Brahms' "Academic Festival Overture." Some inconsistencies in the tempo, an inability of the clarinets to
enter at the same time, a couple of sloppy runs in the flute section—it
didn't take much to pick up seven demerits.

George Washington High School lost points for selecting the very same
competition piece they had used the previous year. And while the first
movement from Beethoven's Sixth Symphony—"The Pastorale"—was melodic enough and easy enough to enjoy, it didn't really challenge all
sections, something the judges looked for. Some parts of the band, perhaps
the weaker parts of the band, had mostly easy going. George Washington
High had to settle for the same score they had earned the previous year: 87
—"Very Good."

As the Thomas Jefferson High School Concert Band took their places
on the stage, the group from Oregon City slipped quietly out the side door.
They would await their turn where they could tune up their instruments,
get their lips loose, and receive their final instructions from their director.

When everyone was ready, Mr. Lesser called them to order. "Well,
People, here we are," he said very quietly. "In about fifteen minutes we
will be on that stage in there to see whether we have really paid the full
price or not. We'll find out if we have a "superior" in us tonight.

"Right now the best 4-A score on the board is Woodrow Wilson's 95.
I'm guessing that Jefferson will be higher than that when they get done in
a few minutes. I'm guessing we're going to have to score a 97 or a 98 to
take State.

"I guess that ought to worry me, but it doesn't. I have not a doubt in my
mind that if each of you will do your very best—remembering all the
things we've learned, listening to each other, watching my direction—we
can do better than that. I *know* we can do it. I promised you we'd do it.
Now we're going to go and do it.

"Clarinets, flutes: keep those thirty-second note runs crisp and clean.
Percussion: you just have to hold the tempo for the rest of us. French
horns: are you ready to knock 'em dead in the *andante*? And Mr. Sherwood: how are you feeling? Can you do it?"

Andrew said nothing, but the expression on his face gave the answer:
he was ready.

"Now, some final reminders. Do not lift your instruments until I lift my baton. Then bring them up crisply and in unison. Do not look at the audience. Do not look at the judges. Do not tap your toes in time to the music. Keep your feet flat on the floor. When you are not playing, place your instruments on your laps, and sit absolutely still, looking only at me or at your music. Watch your posture: I want every one of you to look like officers in the U.S. Marine Corps.

"I want you to *feel* what you are playing. When the music is angry, I want you to feel angry. When the music is moody, I want you to seethe inside. At the end, when the music is bold and aggressive, I want you to be throwing sailors out of bars."

An official appeared at the door. "Oregon City High? Five minutes. You're on in five minutes."

"A last tip: when you are in your seats on stage, take a deep breath and then let it out slowly. Then fill your lungs with confidence and quiet assurance. Let this thought run through your minds: we've paid the price. We've earned it. We can do it. We will not be denied.

"And one thing more: if somehow we don't take a 'superior'—if somehow we don't take State—that's all right, too. Win, lose, or draw, you're my kids, and I love you, and I'm proud of you, and I *know* you're the best band in the state. I . . . I don't need the New York Philharmonic anymore."

As the band members filed onto the stage, they couldn't help but glance at the tally board to see how Jefferson High had done. It was as Mr. Lesser had predicted: Jefferson had earned an astonishing 97 for a "Superior." Oregon City was going to have to be very, very good to take State.

Mr. Lesser walked to the judges' table and distributed to each of the four judges the complete conductor's score for the competition piece he had selected. In amazement, the judges looked first at the title, then at each other. "Shostakovich's Fifth?" one said. "A 1-A high school band is going to attempt the *Finale* of Shostakovich's Fifth in the State 4-A Competition?"

"Either this little band is very good, or they have a very bad sense of humor," whispered another judge to his colleagues.

Scattered through the audience were parents and teachers from Oregon City, plus generations of alums hungry to see the Pioneers finally win *something*. Also present were the police chief and several patrolmen, ready to escort the Oregon City bus on its (hopefully) triumphant trip home. Seated nearby in the auditorium were Doctors Ahrens and Feldman and a number of nurses from the hospital. On the very front row sat Alton Ryckman with Jim and Alice Sherwood. The truth is, with Oregon City being only 13 miles from Portland, just about the whole of Oregon City was present. An air of almost unbearable suspense filled the room as everyone waited for the music to begin.

Ervin Lesser stood before his band, his hands at his sides. Silently, he mouthed the words, "Let's do it! Let's knock 'em dead!"

Then he lifted both hands, and all instruments came up as one to playing position. There was absolute silence in the room.

And then the auditorium was filled with the sound of a *fortissimo* whole note followed by quarter notes resounding from two shiny new tympani. At a rapid tempo—*allegro non troppo*—the cornets, trumpets, and trombones announced the main theme. The entire band answered with four crashing eighth notes exactly on the beat.

At letter A, Carole and Julie and the other high woodwinds got their first crack at the main theme as the lower woodwinds supported them with a steady eighth-note backdrop. Then it was into the woodwind blizzard of thirty-second note runs.

The flutes were magnificent. The clarinets were outstanding. The oboe and the saxes were brilliant. It was not two dozen instruments playing, but *one* instrument being played by three dozen pairs of hands.

At Letter B, the flutes got a rest as the lower woodwinds plunged into the same swirl of thirty-second notes—sounding like nothing less than a howling blizzard right out of Russia. It was sheer perfection.

Through Letter C the magic continued, with the performance getting only stronger. The woodwinds were doing all that a conductor could ask, and they knew it. On past Letter D they plunged, on past Letter E.

One judge realized suddenly that he had become so transfixed by the music that he had failed to even turn the pages of the director's score before him. Another judge glanced to his left and right and saw that none of the judges had, as yet, noted even one demerit.

Approaching Letter F, the mood changed. The volume dropped, and the frantic tempo slowed. A quarter note melody started in the high brasses and then descended into the trombones. Then a fanfare from the French horns announced a *fortissimo* reprise of the new melody, combining at the same time a triplet convolution in the higher brasses.

After all this much noise and intricacy, the quiet, haunting French horn melody introduced at Letter G was a welcome relief. With every low woodwind and every low brass in the band providing whole notes at pianissimo, and with the flutes and first clarinets providing an almost inaudible eighth-note counterpoint, Martin's solo horn sang its infinitely tragic song. (Seated in the fourth row, Mr. Goodmanson recognized this as a reprise of Carole and Martin's physics "term project"—and determined that they would receive "A's" after all.)

One of the judges, a French horn man for sixty years, reached for a handkerchief to wipe tears from his eyes. As he did so, he noted that still there were no demerit marks on any of the judges' score sheets.

The solo ended, the high woodwinds reclaimed the spotlight in a louder, more animated song. The flute, soon joined by a piccolo, carried the melody line as the lower reeds called out again and again, repeating their melodic question.

And at Letter I, Carole Larsen, solo flute, gave them their answer in a ghostly, almost transparent melody. And far, far down the scale her melody was echoed by a confident, controlled baritone sax playing the bassoon part.

A judge reached for his pencil. "Brilliant!" he wrote. "Baritone sax in place of missing bassoon."

Through Letter J, past Letter K the music flowed—incredibly soft, incredibly moody—and executed to absolute perfection. Perspiration poured from Mr. Lesser's face as he led his band, motioning here for a little more, signalling there for a little less, his hands drawing inspired music from his band as a master potter draws a beautiful vase from a mass of clay.

Excitement was building in the auditorium. People in every part of the hall knew that what they were hearing was good—very good. Something incredible was happening as the concert band from small Oregon City High School continued its performance of the *Finale* to Shostakovich's brilliant Fifth Symphony.

At Letter L there came another mood shift. The snare drums and tympani signalled the change with three bars of very soft drum work. Then the low woodwinds picked up the main theme, but at half speed and very softly. Instead of answering with slashing eighth notes on the beat, the rest of the band replied with half notes, sounding for all the world like a mighty organ whispering "Amen, Amen."

Then began a slow *crescendo* of both volume and tempo, with the eighth-note intensity of the lower reeds being emphasized by the half-note main theme being thrown from section to section. Past Letter M the music continued, then past N, building, building, louder, ever more urgent.

A piano and a xylophone entered—not as solo instruments, but as simple percussion, "drums" which could play more than one or two tones. Approaching Letter O, the band began to construct a chord—a monstrous chord which built and built and built toward an unbearable conclusion. The cornets and trumpets sounded the basic minor chord. Then the horns added their note. Two bars later the trombones threw in one more note. Then it was the saxophones. The chord was swelling, building, screaming for some resolution, like a sneeze which has to come, but won't. Incredibly, the basses raised the level of suspense by adding yet one more note to the massive chord.

Mr. Lesser held the chord, held it, held it, and then brought his baton down as the band changed keys and resolved the suspense in the major chord which everyone in the room was waiting for. At *fortissimo* the cornets and trumpet began the main theme once more—but only the first four notes of it! The tympani entered, protesting this distortion of the theme. Again, the high brasses started, and again stopped in a whole note after the first four notes of the phrase. But then they continued on, and the tympani thundered their approval. The horns and the trombones joined in, and finally the whole band.

The end was drawing near. With percussion and high woodwinds providing an eighth-note background, the rest of the band repeated the main theme over and over at half tempo, repeating it over and over again lest anyone in the room should ever forget it.

And then there was the final crashing, smashing chord at triple *fortissimo* as Wally Arnold pounded out the final quarter note exclamation marks on his tymps. The *Finale* was ended.

For a long moment neither the conductor nor his band members moved. For that same long moment no one in the huge audience moved or even breathed.

Then Mr. Lesser lowered his baton to his side, and the auditorium at Thomas Jefferson High School erupted into a mad pandemonium of cheering and whistling and shouting. A spontaneous standing ovation was awarded the little band from the little high school which had provided such a huge performance. Almost immediately, the four judges joined in the standing ovation.

Then the head judge picked up his own paper and those of his colleagues, and saw what he already knew: There were no demerits on any of the papers. Soon the triumphant result was posted on the tally board for all to see: Oregon City H.S. 100—"Superior."

While all of this was happening, Mr. Lesser took his bow, then had his band rise for their bow. Called back again and again by the cheering throng, he had various sections rise and take their bows. Then he recognized his soloists. The tumultuous applause rose to an even higher pitch as Andrew Sherwood, baritone sax in hand, rose and bowed to the audience.

15
The Ends

Well, that's where the story ends.

Oh, except the part where Andrew actually gave Julie a great big hug—right on stage and in front of everybody, and with the television camera recording it all for the ten o'clock news.

Oh, and the part where the judges handed this huge trophy to Mr. Lesser, and he said it was too heavy for him, and could Wall and Chuck carry it for him.

Oh, and the part where Airline and the cheerleaders taped a big red and white banner to the side of the bus which read OREGON CITY TOOK STATE! And on the other side of the bus the banner said OREGON CITY PAID THE PRICE!

The End (again)

Really. That's where the story ends.

Except maybe the author ought to mention that Doctor Feldman kept working with Jim Sherwood. He got him into Alcoholics Anonymous, and he helped him feel better about himself, and that helped his marriage and his relationship with Andrew. And with his not drinking anymore, there was a lot more money for things like clothes for his wife and shoes for Andrew and a telephone for the whole family.

And you'll probably want to know that with the Sherwoods going to church every Sunday, Alice made some good friends so that she wasn't so isolated any more. And pretty soon she and Jim were going out to dinner and going to movies and getting to be good friends with Carole's folks.

Oh, and with Jim Sherwood giving his son so much less to do at home, Andrew was able to take an after-school job working at *The Enterprise*. And that led to some savings, and that led to a 1941 Chevrolet, which Andrew and Chuck and Wall painted red and white.

Oh, and pretty soon Carole was going steady with Martin Strong, and the two of them were going on double dates with Andrew and Julie.

And of course Andrew took Julie to the Senior Prom— where she finally got to wear her formal and her heels—and where Andrew finally learned to dance.

And while we're adding up happy endings, guess who was seen dancing at the Prom with Mr. Lesser: Miss Anderson, the pretty young English teacher!

Let's see, that makes at least one happy ending for everyone, doesn't it? Sounds like a good place to stop.

THE END (Really)

Music Credits

"Mood Indigo," by Duke Ellington, Irving Mills, and Albany Bigard; Mills Music, Inc., 1931.

"But Not for Me," by George and Ira Gershwin; copyright 1930, New World Music Corporation.

"I Don't Stand a Ghost of a Chance with You," by Bing Crosby, Ned Washington, and George Bassman; copyright 1932, American Academy of Music.

"I've Got My Love to Keep Me Warm," by Irving Berlin; copyright 1937, Irving Berlin Music Corporation.

"It Had to Be You." by Gus Kahn and Isham Jones; copyright 1924, Jerome H. Remick & Company.